The Cheese ... Murder

A SLEEPY CREEK COZY MYSTERY BOOK 7

ROSIE A. POINT

Rosie Books

WITH ROSIE A. POINT

Cover by DLR Cover Designs
www.dlrcoverdesigns.com

You're invited!

Hi there, reader!

I'd like to formally invite you to join my awesome community of readers. We love to chat about cozy mysteries, cooking, and pets.

It's super fun because I get to share chapters from yet-to-be-released books, fun recipes, pictures, and do giveaways with the people who enjoy my stories the most.

So whether you're a new reader or you've been enjoying my stories for a while, you can catch up with other like-minded readers, and get lots of cool content by visiting my website at *www.rosiepointbooks.com* and signing up for my mailing list.

Or simply search for me on *www.bookbub.com* and follow me there.

I look forward to getting to know you better.

Let's get into the story!

Yours,
Rosie

One

"IT'S HAPPENING!" AGATHA DUPIN, MY OFT-deranged cousin, burst into my office, disheveled, her hand clutching a velvet pink fedora to her short, plum red hair. "It's happening, Christie! We've got to go."

Outside the office, my assistant, Mindy, was playing her favorite phone game, Sugar Rush or Crunch, or... I couldn't remember, nor did I care. Loud *pings* and congratulatory exclamations came drifting through the doorway *"Oh ho, ho! Sugar CRUSH!"*.

I frowned at my cousin. "Shut the door, will you?" I returned my focus to the case file lying across my desk, or tried to. I had a meeting with my wedding planner in a half an hour, Liam wasn't answering his phone, and it had been nine months since Sapphire Blaze, otherwise known as Special Agent Roberts, had arrived in Sleepy Creek, Ohio, to deliver the "news."

The Somerville Spiders were back. And they wanted me dead.

It wouldn't take much for them to find me. It wasn't like I was in a protection program, so why hadn't they struck yet? The waiting was killing me. As was the humidity in my tiny office in my private investigation firm.

"—happen at last. You've got to come see it."

"Hmm?" I glanced up at my cousin.

She'd shut the office door, but was standing with her hand on the knob, staring at me, urgently. "Didn't you hear what I said?"

"I'm in the middle of something," I sighed, shutting the case file and sliding it across my desk toward my new out-tray. Business had been going well lately, and Liam's pizzeria, Slice of Nice, was a resounding success. "Lay it on me. What's happening?"

"She's finally launched her business." Sweat ran down the sides of Aggy's face, sticking strands of her hair to her pale cheeks. "She's doing it. The washi tape store is gone, and she's opened a... a..."

"Spit it out, Agatha," I snapped, then patted the air. "I'm on edge."

Aggy and Liam were the only people in Sleepy Creek who knew about the impending doom that awaited me and this town if Special Agent Roberts couldn't stop the Somerville Spiders. A sore point for me. I didn't like to sit on my hands while danger was afoot.

"Mona Jonah," she whispered, saying the name like it belonged to a serial killer.

The only thing that Mona killed were the hopes and dreams of those innocent folks unlucky enough to cross her path. And her lawn. She was surprisingly bad at gardening. My theory was that the plants simply gave up on life when she was around. I didn't blame them.

"What's the store?" I asked.

Aggy had gone from my annoying cousin to my right-hand woman and personal assistant. Granted, she wound up in messes I had to extricate her from.

"It's called the Gossip Shoppe."

"You're kidding."

Aggy fidgeted with her puffy khaki shorts. "She's selling gossip. Or collecting gossip. They have coffee."

"Gossip is not a product, last I checked, unless you're writing a column in the local newspaper." And Mona had been fired as the editor of *The Sleepy Creek Gazette.* Served her right for the vitriol she'd printed.

"I think she's doing like, uh, like... what-ya-call-it."

"Ah yes, clear as ever, Agatha. I'll be on the look out for 'what-ya-call-its' on my way to the wedding planner." I got up and grabbed my phone off the desk. Liam hadn't messaged me yet, but if I didn't leave now, I'd be late for my appointment with the wedding planner.

She'd come highly recommended by Grizzy, my best friend, and Arthur, her husband. Truth was, I needed someone to help me plan the wedding because I wasn't the best at organization or the girliest girl around. And girly girl or not, I wanted, desperately, to have a beautiful, memorable wedding like Griselda and Arthur's.

"It's like that thing," Aggy said, following on my heels as I exited the office and nodded to Mindy.

My blonde, college-aged assistant was on summer break and resentful about having to spend it back here in Sleepy Creek. She eyed me up and down and wriggled her nose from side-to-side before returning to her game.

Technically, I didn't need a receptionist. When she wasn't here during the semester, I didn't replace her but answered all my calls, but Mindy's mother had begged for her to come work for me again, and I couldn't turn her down. The woman had dark circles under her eyes and had been losing hair.

I waved to my receptionist and headed out of the building onto the street.

I was just around the corner from the Burger Bar, but I didn't have time for a snack today. I strode down the sidewalk, past trees casting dappled light on the paving.

"Can we go see it?"

"The what-ya-call-it?" I checked my watch. "I have an appointment on Fifth Street."

"That's right where Mona's new shop is," Aggy squeaked.

"Then I guess we'll see it as we walk by."

"It's, uh, it's—do you know that show that everybody watches?" Aggy asked.

"You know I'm not big on TV," I said.

"You know, people my age. It's quite... raunchy, but it's got this woman in it who writes these columns that she prints and delivers to people with the gossip about high society in it?"

"No idea."

"They wear dresses and pretty—"

"Wait, is Mona printing a gossip pamphlet?" I asked.

Aggy clicked her fingers. "Yeah. Yeah!"

"Great. That's great." As if Sleepy Creek needed more drama. I kept walking, peeking my head into the Burger Bar as I passed it by. Grizzy wasn't behind the counter—she'd been spending a lot of time trying to get her baby, Oliver, who was now a whole ten-months-old, into a daycare that she approved of.

The scents of seared meat and melting cheese drifted out, and Aggy lingered in the doorway. I pulled her along behind me, continuing past the corner where Sapphire Blaze usually busked for the locals.

Where was she today? It had been a while since I'd seen Special Agent Roberts, and it worried me.

I took a left down Fifth Street and stopped after a few steps. "What the—?"

"Told you," Aggy said. "It's crazy. I told you!"

A crowd clogged the street, people reading pamphlets and sipping coffees, spilling out of the front of a store with a sign tacked to the bricks above its open doors.

THE GOSSIP SHOPPE *with Miss Mona Jonah, Leader of the Gossip Circle.*

"She's done it again," I muttered, passing a guy who was frowning at the pamphlet. I whipped it out of his hand and kept walking, ignoring his protests. "Pay the man, will you, Agatha?" She disappeared from beside me.

Announcing the FIRST EVER edition of the Miss Mona Jonah Gossip Pamphlet!

"That's not a mouthful at all," I said, and continued walking, ignoring the storefront as I made for the wedding planner's address.

"*Bridgerton.*" Aggy had reappeared beside me.

"Gesundheit."

"No, that's the name of the show. With the woman who has the pamphlet in it. Mona's trying to do the same thing."

"Never heard of it," I said. "But if Mona's doing this, it's only going to be bad news for Sleepy Creek."

I stopped outside the wedding planner's boutique store. An intercom with a brass button was tacked to the side of the building, and the door was made of frosted glass. Vast windows let in light and showed off a calming, cream interior with puffy stools and a walnut coffee table.

I didn't have time for Mona's shenanigans. I had a wedding to plan.

Two

TIME OR NOT, THE PAMPHLET MADE FOR GREAT reading while I waited for my wedding planner, Simone, and my fiancé to appear. Agatha stood near a potted plant in the corner, fiddling with the waxen leaves and examining them closely.

"It's fake," she announced. "One hundred percent fake."

"Your powers of deduction are improving."

Announcing the FIRST EVER edition of the Miss Mona Jonah Gossip Pamphlet!

It's with great pleasure that Miss Mona Jonah, leader of the esteemed Gossip Circle, presents the first ever Miss Mona Jonah Gossip Pamphlet. Miss Mona Jonah has a passion for the truth, and for the freshest and juiciest gossip. You can expect to find both in the monthly gossip pamphlet. Unfold the page for more...

This was sickly fascinating. Also, trust Mona to capitalize on her penchant for gossip.

OUT OF TOWNER OPENS PRE-OWNED CAR DEALERSHIP

You heard it here first, Noel King, a young and handsome man from out of town has decided to settle down in Sleepy Creek and open his very own pre-owned car dealership. King Motors will launch this weekend, with plans to take the county's car industry by storm.

Rumor has it that Mr. King is both single and looking to mingle, and he has an interest in older women. He's fabulously wealthy, coming from a respected family in New York who own a chain of car dealerships. Women looking for the freshest catch heard it here first.

"Freshest catch? He's not a salmon," I muttered.

"Salmon?" Aggy wasn't a seafood fan.

A bell trilled and was followed by a buzz, and my fiancé, Liam, dashing as always with his dark hair and sparkling eyes entered, still wearing his apron from the pizzeria, complete with a splodge of pizza sauce on the pocket, right over the smiling pizza slice logo.

"Sorry I'm late, honey," he said. "It's been a rush this morning. Mona's new store launch is bringing in business like crazy. Turns out, gossip and cheese go together."

"Ew," Aggy said.

I got up and hugged Liam, careful to avoid the sauce splodge. He kissed me on the cheek and swept my hair back from my face. "How are you doing?" His gaze searched mine.

Liam understood the levels of stress I was under. The feeling that I might put my loved ones in danger was a constant weight on my shoulders.

"How's your back?"

I stretched it out, twisting left and right. "Good today," I said. "I slept well last night, mostly because Poirot lay on my stomach and stopped me from tossing and turning."

"Good." He kissed my forehead.

"There's the loving couple." A woman swept into the room, smiling as bright as the sun—blinding and not to be looked at head on. Blonde, with her hair in a chignon, wearing shimmery rouge on her cheeks, and dressed in a smart black pencil skirt and a cream blouse. Well put together with a veneer of fabulous. She had a crumb on the corner of her lip.

She'd forced a hurried snack down before coming out to meet us? Hadn't had breakfast? Why?

Who was she?

Anyone I didn't know personally could be a plant for the Somerville Spiders. Even people I knew could be a part of the gang, a thought that gave me the chills. They could easily have been waiting for the right moment for years, planning my demise.

Liam squeezed my hand and brought me back to the present.

"Nice to meet you," I said. "Christie Watson."

"Liam Balle."

"Agatha Dupin," my cousin said, seriously, and stretched out a hand.

The wedding planner's smooth brow wrinkled. "And which of you are getting married?"

"I will," Agatha said, pursing her lips. "There's no need to pressure me. I haven't found the right candidate yet, but I'm sure he'll show up soon."

The wedding planner stared at Aggy and opened then shut her mouth. The usual reaction to my cousin's lack of social cues.

"Liam and I are getting married," I said. "Aggy's my cousin. She's here for moral support."

Agatha puffed out her chest and adjusted her pink beret. "And for the cake. I heard there'd be cake?"

"We'll get to the cake tasting soon enough," the wedding planner said, her too-bright smile only faltering for a second before she put it back up again. "My name is Simone Ellsworth, and I am delighted to be helping you today. I started this little boutique with my cousin, funnily enough, so I understand having family around."

I doubted her cousin was anything like Aggy. She was truly one of a kind, in the worst and best ways possible. I'd also eviscerate anyone who looked at her askance.

"Bertrand isn't here today," Simone said. "But I'm happy to be of service. Have you two given any thought to your theme? Or any of the details for your wedding?"

Liam and I exchanged a glance.

"Uh," I said.

"We don't want to break the bank," Liam said. "We'd like to take it easy, and have a wedding that's intimate."

Simone's laugh was a chime-like tinkle. "Of course. Of course. Please, take a seat." She guided us toward the cream sofa. Aggy hovered near the potted plant for further examination.

Simone took a seat on an armchair to our left, gesturing to a thick, leather-backed book on the coffee table. "This contains the information you need to plan a beautiful, cost-conscious wedding."

"I like that word," I said. "Cost-conscious."

"We can go through this together," she said. "The

pressing matters we have to work out first are date, venue, music, and menu. And the theme."

"What do you mean by theme? Like the colors?" I asked.

Simone gave me an ingratiating bob of her head. "That's right," she said. "Colors. What do you have in mind?"

I drew a blank again. I spent my time stressing about cases and the deaths of everyone I loved, or the total collapse of order in Sleepy Creek. I hadn't put any thought into the wedding yet. It was the reason we'd opted for a planner in the first place. But I'd have to make choices myself. This was my wedding.

"I like creams and, uh, lavender colors?"

"That sounds nice," Liam said. "I like that too."

"Wonderful," Simone said, with a clap of her finger-tips. "Wonderful. That's a classy choice, and it helps with flower selection." She opened the thick book and began paging through it, showing us images of venues first. We picked a date for next spring and selected a cute farm on the outskirts of town that was both affordable and picturesque. Next were the flowers, which were easy—sprays of lavender and baby's breath.

"And then, the music," Simone said. "You can choose to have a live band for the reception, but that will be expensive. I would think that a quartet for the wedding service, and then a DJ for the reception might be the way to go? Unless you'd prefer a pianist."

My brain was clogged with information.

"Will the flowers be fake?" Aggy asked.

Simone's head snapped up and she turned to her. "Excuse me?"

"The flowers, will they be fake." Aggy minced over, her left eyebrow arched. "Because that potted plant is surely fake."

"Aggy, stop."

"That's not a fake plant," Simone said.

"Ah, if it's not fake, then how do you explain this?" Aggy returned to the plant and snapped off a leaf. She held it up in horror. "Oh. Oh, no. I'm sorry, I thought—"

Simone squeezed her eyes closed for a millisecond. "That's all right. I can assure you that both the potted plant and the flowers at your cousin's wedding will be real."

Aggy hastily dropped the leaf onto the soil in the pot. "I'm sorry," she whispered to the plant.

Simone checked her watch. "We're almost out of time, but I've got homework for you," she said. "I want you to give some thought to the music for the wedding." She tapped a finger to the corner of her lips. "Oh! I've got an idea. A potential music selection for your wedding is putting on a concert by candlelight in the Sleepy Creek

Park tonight. You could hear them live and see if that's the type of vibe you want for your wedding march."

Liam nodded enthusiastically, but my stomach sank. A public place? With my loved ones? That wasn't the best idea with Special Agent Roberts missing and the Somerville Spiders lurking around.

It was a disaster waiting to happen.

Three

MUCH TO MY ETERNAL CHAGRIN, LIAM WAS excited by the idea of going to a concert in the park by candlelight. I would've been too if the circumstances were normal, but they weren't, and he knew that.

We walked back along Fifth Street toward the corner together, past people reading Mona's ridiculous gossip rag. I twisted my copy of the pamphlet in my hands while Aggy kept pace beside us.

"You can't seriously want to do this," I said. "It's too risky."

"Christie, stop," he said, as we reached the corner. He checked both ways then turned to me, taking me by the arms and melting me with his warm gaze. "You have to check in with reality."

"I am fully connected with reality." Sleepy Creek made

it hard, but I was present and accounted for. "You know we're under risk."

Aggy pressed her lips together and hovered nearby, listening. She wouldn't utter a word about the Spiders, because I'd sworn her to secrecy with the threat of kicking her out my private investigation firm, and my old apartment, which was now hers. Aggy's father had left her a small fortune, but she had to study under me first and prove she was capable of looking after herself. He was trying to force her to stay safe while his enemies lost track of her, and I was fairly certain that threat had passed.

Liam drew me into a hug. "We're going, honey," he said. "We are going."

"You can't force me to do anything," I said.

"I'm trusting that you'll come to your senses on this one," he said. "We can't spend our lives living in fear. And you can't control everything either, Christie. Prepare for the worst, but live. Because if you don't, what was all of this for in the first place?" And then he kissed me on the lips. "I've got to get back to the pizzeria. I'll see you at home for dinner and then we can go see the quartet. Griz and Arthur might want to come too."

Nightmare. The last thing I needed was more of my friends under threat.

Liam waved goodbye to Aggy and left me with my

dark and paranoid thoughts. Was it paranoia when the Somerville Spiders wanted me dead?

I grumbled under my breath, checked both ways, then crossed the street and made for the Burger Bar. A burger would hit the spot and keep me from my spiral of dark thoughts.

Aggy caught up to me. "He's right, Christie."

I shook a finger at her. "We're not doing that."

"I'm coming with you tonight," she said, as I pushed the door to the Burger Bar open, the bell tinkling merrily above it. "I'll be an extra set of eyes." And she widened her eyes, owlishly large, and pressed her glasses up her nose.

The interior of the Burger Bar, with its plush vinyl red stools at the counter near the back, its mirror behind it, and the cozy booths and retro-style fittings, was a home away from home. The scents of the burgers cooking made my mouth water, and two of my best friends, Missi and Vee, sat in their usual spot.

They waved us over, and we went to join them, navigating past tables of locals who were gossiping over Mona's pamphlets or eating burgers and fries with greasy fingers.

"Have you heard?" Missi asked, her tone sharp, as I slid into the seat beside Vee, who was on her iPad, tapping away on the screen.

"Heard what?" I set down my crumpled, sweat-streaked copy of Mona's new gossip rag on the table.

"She's talking about that, dear." Vee tapped the pamphlet then lifted it, pinched between two fingers. "Goodness. What on earth happened to this thing? Did a dog chew it?"

I blushed. "No. That was me."

"You chewed it?" Missi gave me a quizzical look. "That's really something I'd expect from Agatha."

Aggy's jaw dropped.

Vee put down the pamphlet. "There's been a lot of talk about Mona's new business." She tapped on her iPad screen. "I'm writing about it in my blog, as we speak."

"Why?" I asked.

"Damage control." Missi nodded thanks to the server, Hedy, who dropped off their orders of this week's special: The Cheese Burger and Loaded Fries combo. Aggy and I ordered two specials and then turned back to the conversation.

"Damage control for what?" I asked. "Did she besmirch your good names again?" I hadn't read the entire pamphlet yet.

"Not in this month's copy," Missi said, ominously, "but it's only a matter of time." She tucked her straight, gray hair behind her ear then picked up a French fry and ate it.

"The best defense is a strong offense," Vee added. Her gray curls were colored a shade of purple this month.

"We're not going to let her get the jump on us," Missi said. "That Gossip Circle has been causing us drama for years, and it ends now."

"You should come to the string quartet in the park tonight," Aggy added, in what had to be her worst decision to date. Was she out of her mind?

"That's got nothing to do with the conversation, dear," Vee said. "But we happen to have tickets already. A gift from a friend."

"By friend," Missi sighed, "she means that hapless veterinarian who seems to have taken an interest in our antique store." Terrible Twos Antiques was stuffed with interesting curios and affordable furniture. The minute I'd been able to afford it, I'd patronized Missi and Vee's store and bought a desk for my office.

"It's not the antique store he's interested in," Vee replied, slyly.

"Don't you start with me, Virginia," Missi said.

"Then you're coming?" Aggy asked, hopefully.

"Remind me to cut up your hats later," I muttered, and stole one of Vee's fries. She was less likely to whack me on the back of the hand.

Aggy opened her mouth to reply, but was interrupted by the tinkle of the bell over the door as a couple entered. A woman with dark curly hair, a lot like mine, entered on the heels of a tall, handsome young man wearing a red t-shirt that bore the logo, **King's Motors**.

That had to be Noel King, the guy Mona's gossip pamphlet had mentioned.

"—understand why you would do this, Elodie." Noel's voice boomed through the diner.

"Noel, please." The woman's voice was soft. "It's my choice. You can't—"

"Some things are more important than what you want. What about your family? What about the people who love you?"

My stomach clenched. Darn this guy and his penetrating tone and pointed words that applied directly to my situation.

Elodie, the pretty young woman, took a step backward. "I'm sorry, Noel. But the answer is no." And then she fled the Burger Bar.

Noel glanced around the diner and raised a hand. "Afternoon, folks." He found an empty booth and settled in, phone in hand and texting.

"What was that about?" Missi asked.

"None of our business," I replied.

"Since when do you prefer to stay out of other people's business?" Missi asked.

"Since I started valuing my peace." And since I had

bigger problems. Like how I was going to keep Missi, Vee, Aggy, Liam, Grizzy and Arthur safe at an open event in the park at night.

Four

THE SLEEPY CREEK PARK HAD NEVER LOOKED AS romantic. Flickering candlelight cast light on the dark wood of the trees, and the raised stage was set with chairs for the string quartet. A cellist, two violinists, and a violist had taken those seats and were playing a concerto which had silenced the crowd.

I struggled *not* to relax, my hand tucked into Liam's. Grizzy sat on my left, Arthur beside her, both of them beaming as they enjoyed the music. Missi and Vee had taken their places behind us, with Aggy beside them.

The music lulled and the gathered crowd applauded. I scanned those gathered, searching for any sign of a threat, my heart beat pounding in the lull between the pieces. Liam squeezed my hand.

"Relax, Christie," he whispered. "Nothing bad is going to happen."

But I couldn't force the tension to leak out of my shoulders, nor did I believe what he was saying. My gut said otherwise, and I had grown accustomed to trusting it.

The lead violinist rose from her seat and gave a bow, then placed her violin bow against the strings, bringing the crowd's applause to a slow halt.

She was familiar, and it took me a moment to place her.

Elodie. That was her name, wasn't it? The woman we'd seen in the Burger Bar earlier today. I hadn't recognized her, and this explained why—I didn't exactly run in circles with musicians.

She drew her bow across the strings and the first chords of Erik Satie's Gnossiennes No. 1 traveled through the park, accompanied by the cello and the viola.

My pulse slowed, the fear I'd felt seconds ago faded away, and my grip on Liam's hand relaxed. I couldn't believe such beautiful sounds could be produced by human beings.

Elodie swayed back and forth as she played the song, but it was almost as if the music was coming from her, not the violin. Her eyes closed, and a smile played across her lips.

"She looks a lot like you," Grizzy said. "Isn't that weird?"

"Just the hair, maybe," I murmured back.

The piece was introspective, almost as if Elodie was questioning herself as she played it.

"What do you think?" Liam asked. "Should we have them play the wedding march for our wedding?"

I nodded.

Elodie raised her bow, and a gunshot rang out.

The violin fell from her fingers and to the ground. Elodie stumbled forward a step, grasping at her chest, and screams shattered the quiet peace in the park. Elodie tumbled forward off the edge of the stage.

I grabbed for Grizzy, but Arthur was already bringing her to the ground. Liam flattened me, lying over my body and shielding it with his own. We had to evacuate.

"Aggy. Missi and Vee," I hissed, looking left.

But all three were already on the ground covering their heads. Others in the crowd ran screaming or were crying for help.

"Get out of here," Arthur said, rising and removing his gun from the holster at his hip. "Call 911. You can't stay here, you're sitting ducks." And then he was off, moving through the crowd and searching for the gunman.

Grizzy wept beside me, and I grabbed hold of her hand and helped her up.

THE POLICE ARRIVED ON THE SCENE SHORTLY after we'd put the call through to 911. Arthur and the other officers secured the area, searching for the gunman but having no luck. Whoever had killed Elodie had done so purposefully. They'd also been a good marksman and made a hasty escape right after.

I couldn't help considering Noel King, who had been arguing with her in the Burger Bar earlier in the day.

Grizzy held my hand. We stood across from the park, waiting for the cops to take our number or our statements. Liam hovered protectively nearby, now that it had been confirmed that this was no longer an active shooter situation.

Aggy, Missi, and Vee, had gone home, and they weren't the only ones. My theory was that the killer had escaped with the rest of the crowd, during the rush of evacuation.

"We should go," Liam said.

"I want to find out what's going on," I replied. "But if you could take Grizzy home—"

"No way, Chris," Grizzy said. "You can't stay here on your own. What if the shooter comes back?"

"The safest place to be right now is surrounded by police. And—"

"Here comes Detective Hardwick," Liam said.

Shoot. I should have left. The detective was full of himself, and he strode over, ruffling his shock of auburn hair. He was Mona's cousin, which meant I was persona non grata in his eyes.

"We meet again, Miss Watson," he said, ignoring Liam and Grizzy entirely. "At another crime scene, I see. You can't help yourself."

"A woman died, Hardwick," I snapped. "Show some respect. About a half an hour ago, we were all fearing for our lives and that's your opener?"

Hardwick's cheeks tinged pink, but he shrugged. "I'm doing my job, Watson. I take it you were here for the concert, correct?"

"Are you taking our statements?"

Hardwick brought a notepad and pen out of his pocket, twisting it so that he could view the page by the light of the lamppost nearby. "I sure am," he replied. "This is no longer an active shooter situation. It's the scene of a murder, and you're hanging around—"

"You're not seriously accusing us of anything," Liam stated, firmly.

Hardwick's gaze danced sideways toward him and away again, too chicken to confront my fiancé directly. He found it easier to try to bully me, but I would free him of that misconception.

"We didn't see the shooter," I said. "Is she the only one who was hit?"

"Who?" Hardwick asked, testily.

"You've got to be kidding me." I took a step toward him. "You know exactly who I'm talking about. The woman who died."

"I'm not at liberty to discuss the details of my case," Detective Hardwick said. "We don't need your help, Miss Watson, in case you get any wise ideas."

"Wise ideas are the only kind of ideas I have," I said deadpan. "Do you need anything else from us? You want to take our witness statements, Hardwick?"

He gave me an impetuous once-over. "Nah. I'm good. Y'all are free to go." And then he walked off without giving me the slightest hope that he could solve the murder.

Five

I SPENT THE NEXT MORNING, A SUNNY AND TOO hot Saturday, seething about Detective Hardwick's handling of the case and his treatment of the people I cared about. He'd been dismissive of Grizzy and Liam, not just me, and while I could take that on the chin, I didn't take kindly to his rudeness toward my people.

Though I had the day off, I spent my time in the office alone, the air conditioning unit struggling, with my yellow legal pad on the desk in front of me.

I tapped my pen in the margin, considering my notes.

> Victim: Elodie Last Name Unknown
> Crime: Committed during a concert in the Sleepy Creek Park. Gunshot to the chest.

Sharp shooter—had to be, given the accuracy of the shot. Return to the crime scene as soon as the police have finished with it. Might be evidence they missed.

I underlined that final line with gusto.

Suspects:
Seen with Noel King on the morning of the murder, arguing.
Notes:
Griselda mentioned that the victim, Elodie, looked similar to me. Could this have been the Somerville Spiders and a case of mistaken identity?

The Spiders were Boston mobsters. Organized crime was usually organized, and I had my doubts about this being a hit gone wrong. It was possible, but not probable. I scratched my forehead, but movement behind the misted pane in my office door drew my attention.

"Who's there?" I called, opening my desk drawer and placing a hand on my pepper spray.

Aggy bustled into my office, breaking the tension with

her frenetic energy. "We're going to be late, Christie. We've got to go."

"This seems to be your favorite pastime," I said, gesturing toward her, pen in hand. "Rushing in and telling me what to do and where to go."

Aggy grinned at me, adjusting today's hat selection atop her red locks—a Stetson again. It was her favorite, in particular because it was large and often drew stares. Though, I was sure that Aggy's motivation wasn't attention. It was being her authentic self.

"Give me a minute. I'll meet you outside," I said.

Aggy gave me a deep, querulous frown then left me alone.

I waited until I was sure she was outside the building before sliding my lower desk drawer open, reaching inside, and removing the false bottom I had installed after I'd bought it from the Terrible Twins.

When Special Agent Roberts had informed me about the Somerville Spiders and their plans for my demise, I'd started making arrangements. To protect my friends and family, I needed the correct hardware—surveillance cameras and microphones and weapons.

I checked that Aggy hadn't sneaked back into the building then removed a black box, the size of my palm, from the hidden compartment. I opened it and removed a tiny camera with a microphone built in, holding it up to examine it.

This was as state of the art as I could afford, which meant, it wasn't that state of the art, but it would have to suffice.

Three other bugs looked up at me from the box, but I returned it to the secret compartment and shut the drawer. I pocketed the bug, locked up, and went out to meet Agatha.

"What were you doing in there?" Aggy asked, as we started our walk toward the twins' antique store.

"That is 'need to know' information," I said. "And you do *not* need to know."

Aggy wriggled her nose, but didn't complain. She regaled me with tales of her evening in the apartment, people-watching from the window and sleeping on the sofa. Even though I'd told her that she could stay there until she could get back on her feet and afford to rent, she refused to sleep in the master bedroom.

Terrible Two's Antiques was a cozy store, and the bell chimed over the door as we entered, greeted by the smell of fresh coffee and wood polish. Missi sat behind the counter, reading Mona's gossip pamphlet with a sneer pulling her lips back.

"Only a matter of time," Missi said. "Only a matter of time." She slapped the pamphlet down. "That Mona's going to pay the minute she publishes something about us."

"And good afternoon to you too." I locked the store's door, and Missi arched an eyebrow at me.

"Since when are you paranoid? There have been plenty of murders in this town," she said. "What makes this one different?"

"Just because there's crime here doesn't mean we should be complacent."

"What's for lunch?" Aggy asked.

Missi slid off her stool and beckoned for us to follow her back out of the antique store and around to the staircase that led up to her shared home with Vee. I loved spending time in their apartment, both because they were entertaining and because it was a change of pace.

"It can't be good for you two to climb these stairs all the time," Aggy said.

"Keeps the joints lubricated," Missi replied, flicking the end of Aggy's Stetson upward. "I see we're in cowboy mode today, child? Heaven forbid you break out the chaps next."

Aggy blushed.

Vee was in the kitchen, baking cookies. A dish of macaroni and cheese was on the counter, the smell of melted cheese wafting over. "Hello, dears," Vee sang happily. "Agatha, darling, won't you start fixing a salad? Ingredients are in the fridge." She pointed to the old monstrosity humming and tapping in the corner.

The twins' kitchen was all wood countertops with melamine floors, and a clock high up on the wall, ticking away, and Aggy dutifully went to the fridge to help with lunch.

"I need to use the ladies' room," I said, giving Vee a greeting hug as I passed her by. The sounds of Missi overseeing Aggy's salad-making followed me down the hall. Instead of dipping into the bathroom, which was across from Vee's room, I walked to the antique table near the end of the hall and removed the bug from my pocket. I dropped it among the flowers in a potted plant, then hit the bathroom before returning to the kitchen.

"—masticating the tomatoes with that knife," Missi said, rooting around in a drawer. "I've never seen anything like it."

"Be nice, sister," Vee said. "She's trying to help."

"If by help you mean making tomato puree, then sure, she's helping."

"Anything I can do to be of service?" I asked.

"Oh no," Missi said, straightening with a glinting knife in hand. "You're worse than she is." She pointed at Aggy with the sharp tip. "A lost cause."

"We're trying to teach Agatha how to cook before she

loses the ability to learn," Vee added, opening the oven to check on the cookies.

"Like you have," Missi said.

"Always a delight." I sat down at the table, but I was privately happy for the reprieve. "What do you two think of the murder?"

Aggy squeaked, but we ignored her. She'd never been good with violence or dead bodies.

"Suspicious," Vee murmured. "Very suspicious."

"Who would shoot someone in front of a crowd?" Missi asked. "Seems purposeful. Like they wanted it to be seen."

"Maybe they thought it would be easier to get away in the rush," I said.

Missi shrugged.

"I don't know about that, dear, but we saw something that might be pertinent to the case."

"And that is?"

Vee smiled and Missi chuckled under her breath. They knew I wouldn't be able to resist getting involved, whether Hardwick wanted me to or not. On occasion, the Sleepy Creek Police Department would ask for my help, but with Hardwick's disdain for me, I was out of luck.

"We saw Simone, the wedding planner, talking to Elodie the day before she passed," Vee said.

"She kissed her on the cheek." Missi showed Aggy how

to grip the knife correctly. "So they must have been pretty close."

"Small world," I said, and then whipped out my phone to check whether the shop was open today. Usually, meetings were by appointment only, but I had an excuse for dropping by. "Guess I know what I'm doing after lunch."

Six

AGGY DECIDED TO STAY AT THE TWINS' apartment and feast on cookies while I walked over to the wedding planner's boutique. Mona's new "shoppe" was closed on a Saturday, which was a surprise given her attitude that gossip never slept. It was a blessing—I wasn't in the headspace to run into her today.

I kept my eyes open and my mind sharp, checking that I wasn't being followed as I walked down Fifth Street. One of my favorite things about Sleepy Creek was how close-knit the community was. Every store had a history, and whenever someone new came to town, it took time for them to become a part of Sleepy Creek, but it was an eventuality. Nobody was an out-of-towner forever.

The Belle Bride Boutique and Wedding Planner store was open.

Simone was inside, talking to a gentleman with wavy brown hair, a pair of tortoiseshell glasses, and a knit sweater vest that was entirely unreasonable in this heat. He looked like a professor of some sort, but there were no colleges in and around Sleepy Creek.

Simone was crying, tears streaking mascara down her cheeks, and she leaned against the man's chest, her shoulders shaking. He patted her awkwardly on the back.

Who was this guy? I hadn't seen him around town.

I pressed the buzzer on the intercom and Simone and the new guy sprang apart. He offered her a pack of Kleenex and she took it, gratefully, dabbing her cheeks before turning to the front of the building with a watery smile.

I lifted a hand.

Simone waved back then excused herself from the conversation and buzzed me in. I entered the calm interior of the boutique, gentle classical music playing in the background.

"—let me know if you need anything," the man said.

"Thanks, Gordon," Simone said. "I'll call you."

He removed a card from the pocket of his neat slacks and handed it to her. Simone gripped it in both hands and nodded, waving goodbye.

Gordon gave me a tight-lipped smile.

"Miss Watson," Simone said. "It's so lovely to see you again." But her voice warbled on the lie.

"I'm sorry to stop by unannounced, but I had to talk to you about the wedding. As soon as possible," I said. "But it looks like I've come at a bad time?"

"No, no," she said, fanning her face. "Forgive me. Just having a moment. I, uh, it's been a rough day."

"Ugh, you're telling me," I replied. "Did you hear about what happened last night?"

Simone's grip on the card tightened. She gnawed on her bottom lip, holding back tears. "Yup," she squeaked.

"Crazy. This town is crazy," I said. "I came by because I wanted to discuss the music choices for the wedding." It was mean to do this, but I had to find out what Simone's relationship with Elodie had been. "You haven't been here for long have you?"

"A few years," Simone managed.

"Ah, lovely, so then you're probably used to Sleepy Creek by now, if anyone can ever be used to Sleepy Creek." I forced a laugh. "Anyway, given last night's tragedy, I was wondering if you perhaps had other string quartets I could check out that—"

Simone burst into tears, bringing both hands to her face and smushing the card against it.

"Oh no, I'm sorry. What did I say?" I rushed over to her, well-aware of what I'd said and hating myself for it, but if Simone was connected to Elodie, there was a chance she'd been involved in her death. I hadn't seen her at the concert last night, and the shooter had to have been there, between the trees.

Though, that wasn't for certain until I'd officially reviewed the crime scene.

I wrapped an arm around Simone's shoulder and brought her over to the sofa. Gently, I removed the card from her clammy grasp and gave it a quick glance.

Gordon Sinclair.
        Psychologist and Counsellor. MFT.

I memorized his name so I could look him up later then set the card down on the coffee table, turning to Simone. "I'm sorry, what did I say?"

"It's that... I was friends with the—with the victim," Simone said. "This was the last thing I expected to wake up to this morning. I can't believe it."

"I'm sorry for your loss." I put my arm around her shoulders and squeezed. "That is so awful. Were you two close?"

"We were best friends for years. Elodie moved to town six months ago, and I feel like if I hadn't suggested she come live here, this wouldn't have happened."

"Oh gosh, you can't think like that," I said. "That's not fair to yourself."

"But it's true. If I hadn't invited her here, she would

never have been in the park last night," Simone continued, wiping tears off her cheeks with her fingertips. "And she would never have— Oh, I can't even deal with this." She covered her face. "I'm being so unprofessional. I think you should come back later when I—"

"There, there," I said, patting her on the shoulder. I was getting better at connecting with people instead of being my usual impulsive and "logical" self. "It's all right. You don't have to be professional. You're doing great."

Simone nodded and gave me a trembling-lipped smile. "Thank you. She was such a lovely, kind person. I don't understand why this happened. All she wanted was to settle down in a cute town like this and play her music for people who would appreciate it. I—"

Footsteps tapped on the polished wood floor, and a handsome young man in a suit entered. "Simone? Oh, no." This had to be Bertrand. He rushed over to Simone's side and took her hand. "Oh, honey. Come on. Come on, now, let's get you freshened up." Bertrand gave me a light tap on the shoulder. "I'm sorry about this, Miss—?"

"Watson," I said, shaking his hand. "Christie Watson."

"Do you mind coming back on Monday?" Bertrand asked. "I think Simone needs time off."

"Absolutely," I said. "No problem. Take care of yourself, Simone."

She didn't look at me as I left but grasped Bertrand's

hand, weeping quietly. The minute I hit the sidewalk, I searched for Gordon Sinclair's practice address.

Seven

THE REST OF THE WEEKEND HAD BEEN PAINFUL,
apart from time spent with Griselda on Sunday, having a
picnic and playing with my godson, Oliver, who was
scooting and standing and had the most adorable gummy
smile—his front teeth had started coming in, and he was
an absolute drool-monster.

Poirot and Curly Fries had their own play date
indoors. "Play date" was code for stand-off from Curly
Fries' side. She had lost weight and was angry, but she'd
always been that way, except when it came to Griselda, and
now, when it came to Oliver as well. She was protective
over him, which was kind of sweet to witness. I had
planted a bug in Grizzy's living room, so I was front and
center for their shenanigans.

Liam was busy in Slice of Nice, Aggy was napping like

she had never slept a night in her life, and I spied on Missi and Vee at my leisure. No threats yet.

When Monday came around, I was itching to get back into the case.

I greeted Mindy on my way into the office. "Any messages for me this morning?"

"Mrs. Fingle claims that her cat food is being stolen directly from her pantry. She wants you to come by and help her find the thief," Mindy said, bright-eyed, likely because she hadn't yet picked up her phone and started gaming.

"Diarize that for me," I said. "For this evening."

"What am I, your assistant?"

"Please?"

"Eh."

"I won't complain about your annoying game sounds for a day," I replied.

Mindy grinned. "You got it, boss."

I plopped down behind my desk and grabbed my phone receiver. I'd found Gordon's phone number online and I had been waiting all weekend for this.

Gordon's receptionist answered the phone in a professional drone. "Good morning, this is Silke, and you've reached the offices of Gordon Sinclair. How may I help you today?"

"Hi," I said, "I'd like to talk to Mr. Sinclair, please."

"And who may I say is calling?" Silke asked, sounding unimpressed.

"I'm his landlord," I replied. "I've got a query about last month's rent payment."

"Oh," Silke said, her tone shifting slightly. "Hold on one moment, please."

She hadn't even asked my name. Too easy. I waited while cutesy music traveled down the line, tapping my fingertips on my desk.

"This is Gordon." His tone was uppity, even judgmental, as he waited for my response. "Listen, Clive, I'm good for the money. I need time. Two more days, max, and I'll pay you."

I filed that away for later. Mr. Sinclair was late on his rent. "Hi Gordon, how are you today?"

"Who is this?" he asked. "You're not Clive."

"No, sir, I am not," I replied. "My name is Christie, and I wanted to ask you a couple of questions."

"If you want an appointment, you can ask my—"

"The questions aren't about counseling or therapy. I want to know what your relationship is like with Miss Simone Ellsworth."

"I don't see why I would share anything with a stranger over the phone."

"I'm a private investigator looking into the death of

Elodie," I said, regretting that I still didn't have the woman's last name. "Does that change your mind?"

"Not particularly. You aren't the police."

"No, I am not. But I often work with them," I said, "and in this case, I'm—"

"Listen, Chesamay, was it?"

That wasn't remotely close to my name. "Christie."

"Whatever. I have an incredibly busy schedule, and if you want to make an appointment with me, you'll have to organize one through my website or my receptionist. Good day to you."

"A second, Mr. Sinclair," I said. "This is important. You—" He hung up, the sound of the dead line ringing in my ear. I could have handled that better, but I doubted Gordon would give me much in person. He hadn't bought my story about working with the cops. I could usually rely on that to help me gather leads. Ethical or not, it worked.

My office door flung open hard enough to rebound.

"What the—?"

Investigator Brown swept into the room, complete with his usual caricature of a trenchcoat, his collar popped, dark, beady eyes fixed on me. "Watson."

"Mindy," I shouted. "Is there a reason you let this man in here?"

"As if I could stop him," she said. "Besides, I'm on a win-streak." The *pings* and exclamations from the game punctuated her words. "You've got to pay me more if you want me to, like, pay attention or whatever."

I swallowed my frustration. "What do you want, Brown?"

He strode threateningly toward my desk and placed those tapered, too long fingers on it. "I think you know, Watson."

"I really don't."

"Oh, but you do."

I pinched the bridge of my nose. Why couldn't he be *normal*? I could handle annoying, but crazy and annoying? I had enough of that in my life. "I don't. So cut to the chase."

"You know."

"Brown," I said. "I'm going to kick you out of my office if you don't start talking."

He pulled himself up straight. "You. Kick me out of your office? I'd like to see you try."

I slid my desk drawer open, removed the pepper spray, and set it down in plain view. "You won't be 'seeing' anything when I'm done with you. Now, spit it out or get out."

Brown's gaze flickered to the pepper spray. He fiddled with his trench coat collar obsessively then cleared his throat. "I want what you've got on Elodie King's death."

My ears nearly perked up at the mention of her last

name. Elodie King. Related to Noel, the car guy? I had googled the name Elodie, but without the last name, I'd found social media profiles and news from around the world. *The Sleepy Creek Gazette* hadn't yet published an article about the death—I expected it would happen sometime today.

"Why on earth would you assume that I know anything about that?"

"Because you can't resist getting involved in things that don't concern you," Brown said.

"HEY HO! You're a winner to go!" The tinny encouragement nearly drove me up the wall.

"Mindy," I called, as pleasantly as I could muster.

"You said you wouldn't complain about my game noises if I added Mrs. Finkle to your diary," Mindy said.

"And did you add Mrs. Finkle to my diary?"

"No, but I could have. That's the point."

"Mindy you'd better turn that game down now before I break your phone in half," I snapped.

Investigator Brown took a step backward at my tone, his gaze darting back down to the pepper spray. "Interesting way to run an office."

"Hey, buddy, you don't get an opinion around here," I said. "And I don't know anything that can help you. Besides, you shouldn't be getting involved in the case either. It's police business."

"Yeah, well, they hired me to help 'em out," Brown said.

Mindy's game cut out in the reception area, and she appeared in the doorway, glaring at the back of Brown's head. "Hey!"

Investigator Brown turned around, hawkish in his movements, his shoulders hunched. "Huh?"

"Get out." Mindy pointed at the door. "Now." Annoying or not, I could count on Mindy to have the company's best interests at heart.

"Excuse me, but—"

Mindy took a step toward him, and she was surprisingly frightening for a short, young woman with raccoon eyes from consistent device use. "I said vamoose!"

Brown cleared his throat a couple of times, sweeping his head from left to right as he took us both in. He squeezed past Mindy and made for the building exit. "This won't be the last time you hear from me, Watson. You mark my words." He cast that over his shoulder.

"And I'll have my pepper spray ready for you the next time you stop by," I called back. "Thanks, Mindy."

She shrugged, lifting her phone again. "It's whatever." And then she went back to her desk, the *pings* and exclamations less annoying than usual.

I settled back into my seat, steepling my fingers underneath my chin, lost in thought. Arthur should have told me that the P.D. was hiring Investigator Brown, but he was busy with the case and he was second to Detective Hardwick. I understood why he wouldn't call me about it. Arhturh was conflict avoidant and I was a ball of "respect me or die" navigating through a world full of disrespect.

But Brown had given me a lead without intending to, and I was going to use it to my advantage. I didn't trust Brown to solve the case, nor could I sit back and watch the cops handle this when it might involve the Somerville Spiders.

And where the heck was Special Agent Roberts?

I brought out my yellow legal pad to note down her name.

Aggy burst into the office building, urgent as always with her hand pressing a flat cap down on her head.

"What is it this time?" I asked. "Surely—"

"Missi and Vee are fighting Mona Jonah! Come quick!"

I leaped out of my chair and grabbed the pepper spray.

Eight

"I TOLD YOU," MISSI YELLED, THE NOISE traveling out of Mona's gossip store and onto the sidewalk. "I'll have your head for this. I will have your head!"

"You've got to calm down, sister," Vee said. "You're going to give yourself a heart attack."

The crowd of gossip enjoyers had gathered on the sidewalk to watch the showdown. Most of them had cleared out of Mona's store, which was decorated in her usual combination of bright pinks and leopard print—furry ottomans, a glass coffee table, pink puffy beanbag chairs, and a counter at the back where coffee was served and sold.

Mona's crimson nails tapped against her mug, and she considered Missi over the rim, steam drifting past her face. "I told you, I have no idea what you're talking about."

"You've been watching us," Missi said. "Invading our privacy."

"We knew you would do something like this," Vee put in, and despite her earlier chastisement of her sister, her voice trembled. "And we were right. We're going to report this to the police, of course, but we want you to realize how serious this is. This invasion of our personal lives, this insistence on spreading gossip and rumors about the good citizens of this town."

"And all of you are participants." Missi swung around, pointing a finger at the watchers. They flinched and stepped back or lowered their gazes. "You should be ashamed of yourselves!"

"I'm going to have to ask you two biddies to leave," Mona said.

"Watch it," I said.

Mona Jonah's green-eyed gaze flickered past the twins and found me. "Got something to say, Watson?"

"You're a gossip-monger," I said. "You have no respect for anyone in this town, and you'd better apologize for calling the twins names."

"Or what?" Mona laughed, throatily. "You don't have power in this town any more, Watson. There's a new investigator, my cousin is the lead detective, and I own everyone and everything. A few words from me, and you're toast."

"Keep dreaming," I said. "Missi, Vee. Let's go."

Missi removed something from her pocket and slammed it down on the counter. "This is yours," she said. "And I'm reporting you. It doesn't matter which detective is in charge in this town. The law is the law."

My stomach sank.

The item she'd slammed down on the desk was the bug I'd placed in the flower pot in the twins' apartment. Darn.

"Let's go," I repeated.

I escorted the twins out of Mona's gossip store and down the street, heading toward my office. Aggy fell into step beside us. She was terrified of Mona and had refused to get too close lest she turn her leopard print ire on my cousin.

"Horrible wretch," Missi said.

"I can't believe the nerve of the woman," Vee said.

"What I want to know is how she got this into our apartment in the first place." Missi lifted the bug between her fingertips, holding it upright. "It's beyond belief."

"She must have a mole," Vee said. "A person she—"

"It's mine." I couldn't lie to them now that they'd found it.

The twins stared at me as if I'd admitted that I was a xenomorph from the hit movie *Alien*. I wet my lips.

"You?" Missi blinked.

"It can't be yours," Vee said. "Surely not."

Aggy didn't let out a peep. We had stopped on the

sidewalk on Main Street, across the road from the spot where Special Agent Roberts usually spent her mornings busking under her cover name, Sapphire Blaze.

This was going to be tough. "It's mine," I repeated, and took the bug from Missi's fingers.

"You're in league with Mona Jonah?" Missi asked.

No wonder they were looking at me like I was a stranger. "No, of course not," I said. "But the bug is mine. I planted it in your flower pot because I wanted to keep you safe."

"What?" Missi scratched her temple.

"Pardon," Vee corrected her sister, absently.

"Why?"

"Sleepy Creek is unsafe," I said. "And I care about the people in my life. My friends. I've planted a bug in Griselda's living room as well." It was better to be honest now that I'd been caught. "And one in my old apartment watching over Agatha."

Aggy tugged her flat cap down to shade her eyes.

"You're spying on all of us?" Missi asked.

"It's necessary," I said. "I can't trust that you won't become victims of a—murderer."

"No," Missi said. "No, that doesn't make sense."

"There's something you're not telling us." Vee folded her arms. "What is it, dear?"

Aggy pulled her cap even lower, because she was

privy to the truth. That I was protecting them from more than small town murderers. The mob was going to find us soon enough, but Special Agent Roberts had forbidden me from telling anyone but Liam and Aggy. It was torture. I didn't like keeping things from my best friends.

"Nothing," I said. "That's the reason."

"You're lying," Missi replied. "I can always tell when you're lying, Watson, because your voice goes flat and even."

"Soulless," Vee added.

"Gee, thanks."

"Give me that." Missi snatched the bug out of my hand, threw it down on the concrete, and crushed it under her heel. "You don't get to spy on us or watch over us, if you won't tell us what's going on. Fess up, Watson."

"Oh dear," Vee whispered, clasping her forehead. "Oh dear, Missi."

"What?"

"We accused Mona for nothing. We were wrong," Vee breathed.

"Watson." Missi glared at me. "We'll never live this down. You'd better tell us what's going on."

I looked from Missi's face to Vee's and back again. "I'm sorry," I said. "I can't do that."

"Then, consider yourself uninvited to all friends and

family events at our home until further notice," Missi said, and stormed off, low heels clicking on the sidewalk.

"We don't associate with people who lie to us," Vee agreed, and followed her sister.

And I was left with a crushing sense of disappointment that I had messed this up, once again. Aggy remained beside me and followed me back to the office without a word.

Nine

"Don't worry, Christie," Aggy said, and gave me a pat, pat, pat on the shoulder. "It's going to be okay." My cousin had been treating me like a wounded bird since our run-in with the twins this morning.

I appreciated the support, since it felt as if I'd lost two of my best friends, but it wasn't helping me focus on what I could control. And that was investigating this case. Running after Missi and Vee, apologizing, and begging, would only anger them further. They wanted answers that I couldn't give, and until I reached the point where I could give those answers, I wouldn't convince them to trust me.

It stung like heck.

"Do you want to go to the Burger Bar and get the Cheese Burger Special?" Aggy asked, her tone pleading.

It was lunch time, and my dear cousin was governed by two things. Her stomach, and her choice in hats.

"I'm good, thanks," I said. "But you can run out and grab a bite if you want to. I don't think the twins are mad at you." And I didn't particularly feel like an awkward conversation with them in the Burger Bar, or their frustrated stares.

Gosh, if only I could control this situation. Where the heck was Special Agent Roberts?

"Thanks, Christie!" And then off she went, plastering the flat cap to her head as she hurried out of my office.

Mindy was in there as per usual, her game *pinging* and congratulating her—the ultimate dopamine hit, since everyone needed validation in their lives. Aggy had forgotten to close the door behind her, and I didn't bother asking Mindy.

I shut it and went back to my desk, considering what had happened and what I had discovered thus far.

Elodie King was Noel's relation. Either a sister or his wife? But no, Mona's gossip pamphlet had claimed that he was single, and while I would rather take my chances in a pit of vipers than spend time alone with Mona, when it came to gossip, I trusted her.

Simone had been friends with the victim, and I was curious about Gordon Sinclair's connection to her. He might have information about their relationship I wasn't privy to. As for other suspects? I wasn't sure who might have wanted Elodie dead.

Another person from out-of-town? A Somerville Spider?

That last thought was my anxiety talking. But it was a possibility I had to consider, especially with Roberts missing in action.

I searched up the number for Noel King's car dealership then punched it into my phone.

"This is King's Motors," a woman answered the phone. "How may we help you on this kingly day?" Her tone was saccharine.

"I'd like to talk to the King himself, if possible," I said. "It's about Elodie."

The receptionist let out a breath. "I—Just one moment, please." A jingle played through the phone.

"Have the kingliest of days at King Motors.
At our dealership we're your greatest
    promoter.
Because every king deserves their queen.
At King Motors we keep our prices lean."

"Wow," I muttered. "That's awful."

The line clicked, and a man cleared his throat on the other end. "Who is this?"

"Is this Mr. Noel King?"

"Now, you know good and well it's me," he replied, "since you asked for me by name. I'll tell you what I told every other idiot who comes waltzing in here asking me questions about Elodie. I didn't know the girl."

But he'd been in the Burger Bar with her the other day. "You're not related?"

"Honey, I don't know how to break this down for you in a way you'll understand. Just because two people have the same name, doesn't make them related."

What a delight. "Yeah, I'm aware of that Mr. King. I saw you with her in the Burger Bar a couple of days ago."

"You must have been hallucinating, because I have never been in a 'Burger Bar' in my life. And I never got the opportunity to make Elodie's acquaintance either. Good day to you."

"Mr. King, I—"

He hung up.

People in Sleepy Creek were less willing to talk of late, and I didn't blame them. The world was going to heck in a hand basket or it felt that way.

I pinched the bridge of my nose. Mr. Noel King had elevated himself to the top of my suspect list. Why deny that he knew her if he'd been in the Burger Bar with her, arguing. Not only had they met, but they'd had a long-standing relationship. You didn't fight like that with a stranger.

A knock tapped on the misted glass of my door.

"Come in."

Grizzy entered my office, carrying a takeout box from the Burger Bar. "I thought you might want lunch," she said, with a radiant smile. Grizzy couldn't help being kind. It was in her DNA.

"Thanks," I said, and accepted it from her. "You didn't have to do that."

"Aggy came in and told me that you and the twins weren't talking."

Darn it, Agatha. "It's not a big deal. Just a minor disagreement."

"That's not how she made it sound. And I haven't seen them this morning," Grizzy said, taking a seat on the rickety chair I reserved for my clients. It was comfy but squeaked when you turned it too much to the left. "You know what they're like, Chris. They spend half their day in the Burger Bar when they can."

"Yeah."

Grizzy interlaced her fingers and placed them against her stomach. She'd already lost the baby weight, a feat I admired but couldn't pull off if I were her. Shoot, not that I'd ever have a baby. That was a journey for which I wasn't yet equipped.

"You're not going to tell me what's going on?" Grizzy asked. "I thought we were besties."

"We are besties, Griz."

"Okay, so what's going on?" Her blonde brows drew inward. "I don't get it. You guys argue on occasion, especially you and Missi, but to not be talking at all? That's not like you."

"It's a misunderstanding. They'll come around."

"A misunderstanding about what?" Grizzy asked.

"I—I don't want to talk about it," I said, because then I'd have to reveal that I'd bugged her house too, and that would be mortifying. I didn't regret surveilling my friends. I had to do something to control the danger. This was what was best for them, especially since Roberts didn't want them informed.

"Okay, Chris." But Grizzy was disappointed. "I'll talk to you later."

I held the Burger Bar box after she'd left tapping my thumbs on the top. I wanted to tell them the truth, but I was afraid of what they'd think. I'd put them through enough, they didn't need more danger, especially not Grizzy with her perfect family.

Ten

That night...

"YOU UNDERSTAND HOW IMPORTANT THIS IS," I said to Agatha. "You do exactly as I say, you keep as quiet as humanly possible, and if you have any questions... Well, don't."

"Don't have any questions?" Aggy pulled her black beanie down over her forehead, staring at me through her owlish glasses.

"That's a question, Agatha."

"Oh!" Aggy pulled her fingers across her lips and twisted at the corner. "I won't say a word."

This evening's plan could go either of two ways. Pure

success or unmitigated disaster. I was leaning toward disaster, given that Aggy was sitting in the passenger seat of my cherry red Corvette, trembling with excitement.

We were both kitted out in black clothing—I'd had to stop my cousin from leaving the house and make her change out of the massive sun hat she'd put on for our reconnaissance mission. Aggy's nervous energy was infectious, but I was determined to not let her get to me.

I'd parked the Corvette down the street from the entrance to The Sleepy Creek Park a half an hour ago. The gates to the park were open, but had they been locked I would have scaled them. The police line was gone, which meant Hardwick was done with the scene, or he'd neglected to do his job properly. Either was possible.

If I couldn't protect my friends from the Spiders, I could protect them from the murderer by finding them.

"When do we go?" Aggy asked.

"Yet another question."

"Oh!" Another zipping of the lip. "Sorry."

"You're not supposed to talk after you've zipped your lip."

"Zipped my lip?" Aggy asked. "What's that?"

"That thing you're doing." I zipped my lip. "That's zipping the lip."

"No. That's locking my lips. With a key."

"Same principle," I said, pinching the bridge of my nose. "When we get out of this car, you follow me exactly. You keep silent." It was like the fifteenth time I'd given her these instructions, but with my cousin more was always more.

"And then we're going into the park," Aggy said. "To search for evidence."

"Gloves." I gestured for Aggy to give me the pack of surgical gloves I'd tucked into the glove compartment. It was hot inside the car—I didn't have air-conditioning.

"Hats!"

"What?"

"I thought we were saying our favorite item of clothing," Aggy said. "Yours is gloves and mine is hats."

Please, give me the patience to deal with her tonight. I sent up the prayer. "No," I replied. "No, Agatha, there's a box of gloves in the glove compartment. Please, could you hand them to me, so we can put them on and not contaminate the crime scene?"

"Oh, well, why didn't you say so?"

"I did say so," I replied, with the patience of a saint. Maybe I was ready for children. "Please could you pass me the gloves, Aggy?"

"I thought we weren't supposed to ask questions," Aggy said.

"I swear, if you don't hand me those gloves right now,

I'm going to turn this car around and take you home. And you won't get a treat after lunch tomorrow."

Aggy scrambled the gloves out and handed them to me. "Sheesh. You didn't have to get angry."

I snapped on my gloves and gave Aggy a pair, watching as she pulled them on. "Follow," I said. "Quietly."

We walked down the sidewalk in the muggy night, Aggy close on my heels and occasionally stepping on them. "Not that close," I muttered, and she backed up a pace or two.

I entered the park and walked on the winding path that led through it. Sleepy Creek's park was green from constant care, with trees that towered toward the heavens, older than some of the buildings in town.

I guided my cousin toward the crime scene. A tiny swatch of police tape hung loose against a tree, limp in the breezeless evening.

This was the spot. I checked both ways, searching the darkness for any sign of others in the park, but we were alone.

"Keep an eye out for anyone coming along the path," I whispered to Aggy. "If you see anything, whistle."

"Got it." Aggy gave me a thumbs up.

I hoped she was being honest. I walked between the trees and positioned myself where the stage had been on the night of the performance. I closed my eyes and envisioned the scene that night. The music flowing through the space. The candlelight. It was a miracle nobody had toppled a candle and set the park on fire.

The victim had been standing exactly where I was now. She clutched her chest and stumbled. I mimicked the movement, but a stumble forward didn't mean she had been shot from behind. The bullet's impact hadn't jerked her body.

A lower caliber bullet?

If the person had been a marksman, then they might have used a rifle from a distance. I turned around and walked toward the copse of trees behind where the stage had been and began my search, turning on my flashlight on my phone.

The bark on the trees was rough to the touch but unscarred.

Dustings of wood lay at the base of the tree directly in line with the stage's position on the night of the murder. I ran my flashlight up the tree and found a tiny nick in the wood. A bullet had grazed it. I couldn't possibly tell what caliber it was without a shell-casing, but it gave me a direction to work with.

I marked it out as carefully as I could manage—this wasn't accurate as I didn't have a forensics team specializing in ballistics, but it would have to work for my purposes.

The shooter had been standing across from the stage and their victim, diagonally.

I traced my steps back along that line. The path to the stage was clear, with nowhere to hide. I highly doubted that the shooter had stood in the open. Arthur was a detective. He had been on the look out for the shooter, and Liam and I hadn't spotted anyone suspicious.

I'd been scanning the place the entire night, anticipating a possible attack by the Somerville Spiders.

The shooter had to have had cover. I traced the line even further back until I crossed the path, passing Aggy whose gaze was glued to the far entrance to the park. The best place to hide along this line was behind a tree, near a small lake and a bench, with a clear shot of the stage.

I bent down, setting myself up behind the slats of the bench and pretended to take aim with a rifle.

Had to have had a scope?

A chill ran down my spine while standing in this spot, which might have very well been the killer's hiding place. There was an easy escape—circling the lake and heading for a second entrance nearby. I'd figured from the accuracy of the shot that the murderer had been either ex-military or a practiced shooter. This confirmed it.

And it gave me my next lead.

Eleven

The following morning...

THE SLEEPY CREEK SHOOTING RANGE WAS
outside of town, which meant Aggy and I had spent a
sweltering drive over, the windows open to let in what
barely passed as a cool breeze. I wasn't sure why it was this
hot this summer, but it certainly encouraged me to pick up
more work so I could afford to fix the air-conditioning in
the Corvette.

Aggy wore that sun hat she'd been determined to put
on the night before. It cast shade over my side of the seat,
but I was done complaining.

The shooting range was our next lead, and I was confident we would find what we were looking for there.

Missi and Vee hadn't answered a text I'd sent them, and Grizzy had been subdued. Liam was busy at the restaurant, so my only company last night had been Poirot, who had curled up against my side, peered at me with his wise eyes and purred.

Thank goodness for cats.

"This is it," I said, taking a turn off onto a dirt road. The Corvette bumped along it, the rattle enough to shake my cheeks. We passed a long line of trees that bordered a sunlit field until we finally came to a low white building. A sign out front bore a logo with a target on it, and the words "SLEEPY CREEK SHOOTING RANGE."

What felt like ages ago, I'd visited the gun club with Missi, but this was a different spot, though I'd bet that a lot of the patrons were the same.

We got out, dirt crunching underfoot, and made for the glass sliding doors.

A curvy woman sat at the reception desk, her hair in a buzz cut, a pair of aviator sunglasses stacked atop her head. "Morning, folks," she said. "If you're here for target practice with Coach Dane, you can sign in there." She tapped a clipboard with a sheet attached to it. "If you'd like to hit the range, we're fully booked at the moment, but I can slot you in for the afternoon."

Aggy checked out the roster. She gestured at me, frantically, but I waved her off.

"Actually," I said, "I'm a private investigator from Sleepy Creek."

"Oh, yeah, I know who you are," she said. "Name's Francine Finkle." She got up and stuck out a pudgy hand. "Nice to meet you in person. Most people call me France or Franci. Pick your poison."

"Nice to meet you Franci," I said. "Christie Watson. This is my cousin Aggy."

Franci nodded to Aggy who was jostling on the spot like she needed the bathroom.

"I heard about you two," Franci said, and her tone wasn't unpleasant—a nice reprieve from the reactions I'd been getting lately. "Figured somebody related to law enforcement would eventually pop by, what with the shooting and all."

"Detective Hardwick hasn't come out here?"

"Not yet," she said. "But from what I heard, whoever killed that girl knew how to shoot, and this is where the best shooters in the county hang out." She puffed up then deflated. "Not sure whether I should be proud of that or not any more." She ruffled that buzz cut. "You working with the cops?"

I considered lying to her, but she was an open book, and I'd been hiding enough from people over the last nine months. "Nope. I'm independent," I said. "They're working with Investigator Brown."

Franci snorted. "That old hack? Why?"

"Politics," I said.

"Figures." Franci blew a raspberry. "Dumb thing to do if you ask me. My sister hired him to find her missing cat food and he failed."

"Hey, wait, your sister's name is Mrs. Finkle? She was my most recent client."

"Yeah!" Franci said. "She was impressed how quick you found that cat food."

"Thanks." I smiled.

She gave me an open grin back, and my shoulders relaxed. Franci had good energy, while Aggy had the energy of a golden retriever who had found a slime-coated stick and was desperate for my attention.

"What do you want to know?" Franci asked.

"Can you keep a secret?"

Franci walked back a step and checked through the doorway that led into the office. "Do you play dead when attacked by a bear?"

I opened my mouth to follow up with a question about my suspects, but Aggy interrupted. "It depends on the bear."

"It was a rhetorical question, Aggy," I said.

My cousin shifted her weight from her right foot to

her left. "Yeah, but if you play dead with a polar bear it will eat you anyway. They're the only bears who see humans as food. They see everything as food."

"You an ursinologist or something?" Franci asked.

Aggy pressed a hand to her chest. "Excuse me? Urinologist? How dare—"

"Anyways," I said, before we got sucked into another of Agatha's tangents. I loved my cousin, but she had a tendency to draw attention away from the topic at hand because of the way her mind worked. "I wanted to ask about your regulars. I have a list of suspects, and I'd like to cross-reference them with members."

"Sounds like fun," Franci said, and sat back down behind her desk. "I can bring up our member list and the register of people who've been shooting at the range over the past month, if that will help."

"It sure will."

Franci beckoned for me to join her, but Aggy cleared her throat repeatedly and grabbed the sign up sheet for the coaching. She tapped it with her fingernail and thrust the clipboard toward me.

I took it from her, giving Franci an apologetic smile.

Jason Wilkes
Deborah Mason
Bob Billings

Simone Ellsworth
Devon Barkshire
Gordon Sinclair

My eyebrows lifted. Two of the suspects were here. I slid the clipboard toward Franci. "What can you tell me about these two?" I gave Aggy a thumbs up and my thanks. Guess we'd be getting treats after lunch today.

Franci read the names I'd mentioned and gave a knowing nod. "These two? They're here all the time, separately, though. I'd say Simone has a lot of experience shooting, but not nearly as much as Gordon."

"And what about Noel King?" I asked. "He ever come around here?"

"The car dealership guy?" Franci wriggled her nose. "Nope. Haven't seen him when I've been on my shift." She typed on the keyboard and squinted at the computer screen on the desk. "Nah, I don't have him on record on here either. He doesn't shoot, not here, at least."

"Thanks, Franci. This is helpful. What type of guns do Simone and Gordon usually shoot."

"Oh, it varies, but they're both great shots. They shoot rifles, pistols, and shotguns. Depends what they're in the mood for, but that's the case for a lot of our shooters. People come here to unwind after a long stressful day at work."

"Thanks, Franci. Can I call you if I need more information?" I asked.

"Any time," Franci said. "I appreciate what you do for this town, Christie. Sure made my sister's life easier." She wrote her name and number on a sticky note then tore it off and handed it over.

"I'll be in touch if I need anything," I said, and lifted a hand in greeting.

Aggy and I walked out of the range together. "You're not going to spy on them?" Aggy asked. "Gordon and Simone?"

"I have what I need here." My next task would be to get their alibis. They could shoot, sure, but where they were on the night of the murder was pertinent. I couldn't find the killer without that connection.

Twelve

LATER THAT AFTERNOON, I MET UP WITH LIAM outside the wedding planner's boutique. My heart skipped a beat when he turned the corner and came toward me, and I scanned the street and the buildings across the road, searching for danger.

Mona's gossip store was open, though there were less crowds today. Gossip Circle regulars were inside, wearing their favorite pink jackets bearing the words "Gossip Circle" across the back, and leopard print tights.

I doubted any of them were Spiders, but I couldn't be too careful. Sweat beaded on the back of my neck.

I'd dropped Aggy back at the office with the strict instruction to eat her cookie and to stay away from strangers. Ridiculous, given my entire business was based on talking to strangers, but panic had started setting in.

Missi and Vee were unreachable. I had a view of Grizzy's living room on my phone—a cloud app that provided me with the live feed from her house—but the most I'd witnessed this morning was Curly Fries hacking up a furball.

"Hey, honey." Liam kissed me on the cheek then pulled back and wiped his mouth. "Uh... you're a little bit hot?"

"Sorry." I grimaced. "Yeah, I'm sweaty. It's not the heat. I was worried something had happened to you."

"Chris, come on," he said. "If they were going to attack us, don't you think it would have happened by now?"

"No? They waited years before they tried to take me on the last time. They burned my mother's house down. There's no knowing what they're planning or what they're capable of. I wish you and Aggy would get that already."

Liam drew me into a hug and squeezed. "You can only prepare as best you can. Other than that..."

I pushed out of the hug, though it had been much-needed. "Yeah, well, I don't buy that, nor do I want to. I've tried to plan but people keep getting in the way."

"What do you mean?"

I wet my lips and glanced down at my sneakers. Hot in this weather but better for investigation work when I was on the go. "Missi and Vee aren't talking to me."

"Why?"

I sniffed.

"Why, Christie?"

"Iplantedamicrophoneintheirflowerpot." The words were a whispered, mushed up hiss.

"You planted a microphone in their flower pot?" Liam nearly shouted it.

"Shush!"

"Sorry," he said, glancing around. "But that's crazy, Christie. I get why they wouldn't want to talk to you. But, wait, Missi and Vee are understanding. Tell them why you did it."

"And admit that I've endangered their lives?" I asked.

"What's more important? Your pride or your friendship with them?"

I hated when my fiancé made fantastic points. "I don't want to lose them as friends, but I hate that I've done this to them."

"This is not your fault, honey." He ran his hands over my shoulders and down my arms. "This is not even your mother's fault. This is *their* fault."

The Spiders. He was right, but it didn't make this any easier.

Bertrand appeared in the glass windows of the wedding planner's boutique and waved at us. He let us in on a cloud of his cologne and we were immediately doused in his effusive welcome.

"How lovely to see you two," he said. "You were here the other day, right?" He pointed a finger at me with an excited smile. "Working with Simone?"

"Yeah, I don't think we were officially introduced. Christie Watson."

"Liam Balle."

"Wonderful," Bertrand said. "I believe Simone mentioned me before, but I'm Bertrand. I have news. It's not the best news, but it's not the end of the world either."

"Oh," I said.

Liam took hold of my hand and squeezed. I appreciated the support, because I didn't need extra stress on my plate. I had Aggy, Missi, Vee, Oliver, Grizzy, and Arthur to worry about. Throw in Poirot and Curly Fries and I was maxed out.

"Simone is taking a leave of absence, so I'm taking on all her clients. I understand you just started working with her, correct?"

"That's correct," I said.

"I have your custom wedding book right here," Bertrand gestured to the coffee table. "In it, Simone has placed all your current requests, thoughts and ideas, as well as a moodboard for the wedding. Would you like a cappuccino while browsing through it together and coming to a few conclusions?"

"That would be great," Liam said. "Thanks."

Bertrand's smile became fixed as he scanned my dashing fiancé from head-to-toe. "You can feel free to leave that, uh, apron, is it?"

Liam touched his stained apron from Slice of Nice. He'd rushed over from work again. "Yeah. I'm the owner of the pizzeria."

"Wonderful. That's just wonderful." Bertrand forced it out. "You can hang the apron up on the coat rack over there. Might make you more comfortable." And then he hustled off to prepare our cappuccinos at a state of the art machine in the corner.

Liam held back a laugh as he removed his apron and hung it up, winking at me. I giggled.

Trust Liam to put me in a good mood.

Bertrand came over shortly after with a silver tray bearing two cappuccinos. He set them on the table, then sat in the armchair Simone had taken when we'd had our first appointment here.

"I'm so sorry about what happened to Simone," I said.

"Happened to her?" Bertrand's eyes rolled upward. "I wouldn't go that far. She lost a friend, but, uh, Simone's always been on the dramatic side. Besides, they barely hung out. And she certainly talked enough smack about Elodie behind her back."

Bingo. I placed my hand on Liam's thigh and squeezed in case he had any plans to interrupt or direct the conversation toward the wedding, but I shouldn't have worried. My fiancé was tight-lipped. Besides, he'd lived with me long enough to know when I was in sleuthing mode.

"Wow, really?"

"Oh, yeah. I'm sure they were friends, but if you ask me, Simone is overdue for a break and this was just an excuse for her to take it. Poor thing works herself to the bone."

"Ah," I said. "That's unfor—"

"But she'll be back soon enough, once the dust has settled. She's Type A, workaholic. Miss Thing can barely stand a nap let alone a prolonged vacation." Bertrand tittered a laugh. "Listen to me getting carried away with gossip. Anyway, let's get back to the matter at hand."

And then he turned his attention to the book and flipped it open, showing the lavender and cream-themed moodboard that Simone had prepared for us.

"Now," Bertrand said, "have we decided on a cake or a band? Or a menu?"

"We were hoping to have the Burger Bar cater the wedding," I said.

"The Burger Bar." Bertrand sounded revolted. "I

mean, yeah, of course, the Burger Bar. Who doesn't love burgers at a wedding?" An awkward laugh. "What about the cake? I'm assuming you don't want that to be made out of meat?"

I wasn't bothered by the ribbing. I needed to focus on the case, first, and Simone's "dramatics" were up for investigation.

Thirteen

I KISSED LIAM GOODBYE OUTSIDE THE BOUTIQUE. As a couple, we weren't big on public displays of affection, but lately, I'd needed that extra reassurance. It was unlike me, but Liam loved me and was willing to adapt to what I needed in our relationship. I would do the same for him.

"I'll be home late again tonight," Liam said. "They say the first two years of a business are when it's most likely to fail."

"You don't need to excuse yourself, honey," I said. "I understand how important this is to you, and I've been busy myself."

Liam pressed another kiss to my forehead. "I'll come by your office with a pizza later. Sound good?"

"Sounds great. Bring two. You know what Aggy's like."

"I'll make that three then," Liam laughed.

I waved goodbye then checked my phone for messages from Aggy.

> Where are you? I'm hungry.

>> I'll be back at the office soon. Did you hear from the twins?

My text went unanswered. Three dots appeared and disappeared repeatedly.

>> Aggy? Answer the question.

> Yes, but they don't want to talk to you. I'm sorry. And Grizzy is upset too. She knows about the bug.

>> Great. That's just fantastic.

> 😭😊

>> What's that last emoji for?

> I'm hungry.

I rolled my eyes and started tapping out my response, but my gaze drifted toward Mona's gossip store. A commotion was taking place inside. The members of the Gossip Circle, in their pink jackets and matching sunglasses, were gathered around a center table.

My curiosity got the better of me, as it often did, and I stalked across the street toward the store.

Music drifted out from inside, a classical, familiar tune. My stomach flipped as I put two and two together. It was the same piece Elodie had been playing on the violin when she'd been shot.

Gnossiennes No 1. by composer Erik Satie. It was a haunting tune, nearly overrun by the frantic chatter in the store.

I sat down on a cushioned bench that had been set up underneath the window. Two women were beside me, reading the gossip pamphlet.

"Can you believe it?" the first woman whispered. "Delia, they have to publish another edition this month."

"They're leaving money on the table if they don't," Delia replied, fluffing dark curls. "Gosh, she's really good at gathering the inside scoop, don't you think?"

"It's scary. What if we're next?"

Delia patted her pamphlet against her lap. "That's why we're here. Better to be at her side than in her sights, if you ask me."

Sounded a lot like being the right hand of the devil, though maybe that was an unfair comparison. Mona was awful, but devilish? I considered it, wriggling my nose from left to right. Eh. They might be onto something.

"What's the news?" I asked, casually.

Delia leaned forward. "Apparently, there's been an incident at the Terrible Twins antique store. We're not sure what it is yet, but Mona said that they're about to be exposed in a big way."

"Is that so?" I couldn't help feeling guilty. Sure, Mona might have taken aim at the twins on a regular day, but their outburst in her store hadn't helped. And that was my fault. If I hadn't planted that bug...

Gordon Sinclair entered the store and walked directly toward the center table, a folder tucked under his arm.

The crowd parted to admit him, and I caught a glimpse of Mona, coffee cup in hand, looking like the queen of the world. She gave Gordon a flattering smile, and I held still, lowering my head so she wouldn't notice me, but studying her from beneath my brow.

"Gordon," she said. "I've been waiting for you. Do you have any news?"

"I'm afraid I do."

"Is it about Elodie?" A Gossip Circle member piped up and received a death stare from Mona.

Gordon gave an awkward laugh. "Why on earth do you think I'd know anything about that?"

Quiet filled the store. The melody rushed in to fill it.

Gordon cleared his throat. "I have something good for you today, Mona. I hope you've got something for me?"

Mona gave Gordon a simpering smile, and the chatter started up again. "You bet I do, Mr. Sinclair. It's in the back. I'll come with you to get it." Mona rose from her seat and beckoned for Gordon to follow her. She led him past the counter with the coffee machine and waiting barista and into an office. I glimpsed pink velvet wing-backed armchairs before the view was cut off by the slamming of the door.

What was that about?

"What was that about?" Delia asked.

"Where do you think she gets her gossip from?" The friend sniffed. "Not exactly ethical if you ask me. He's a therapist or a counsellor or something, isn't he?"

"I'm sure he's not giving her confidential information about his clients. That would be illegal."

"I wouldn't put it past him. I heard he's a money-grubbing piece of work. Catherine told me he used to yawn during their sessions and time them so closely that she felt anxiety whenever she went to see him."

"Catherine's always been eccentric, though."

The conversation faded out, but the seed had been planted. Gordon, the counsellor, was trading information with Mona. But what was she offering him? He'd also connected with Simone.

I rose from my seat and walked out of the store before a Gossip Circle member spotted me and decided to report me. Likely, they had already noticed me, but I didn't need a confrontation.

The walk back to the office was filled with rumination about the case and Mona's involvement with Mr. Sinclair. I didn't trust either of them, but that didn't mean they were murderers.

Mindy was at her desk as usual and waved a hand when I asked if I had any messages. That was code for "no" or "yes" or any combination of outcomes.

Aggy was on her favorite stool in the corner, notepad in her lap.

"Working on the case?" I asked, taking my place at the desk. I smoothed my fingers over it. Missi and Vee were going to kill me if they found out why I had bugged their place. They'd kill me for not telling them.

"Huh?" Aggy looked up. "No, I was planning my first cookie for the bakery. I want to make a citrus cookie with a cream cheese drizzle."

I pulled a face. "That sounds fragrant."

"It's going to be the best. Trust me. I'm going to bake them for you tonight!"

"I—"

A text blipped through on my phone, saving me from breaking my cousin's heart when I told her that I had no interest in eating bitter, citrusy cookies.

Help!

My body flushed hot, from the top of my head to the tips of my toes.

The message was from Griselda.

What's wrong?

No answer.

I pulled my laptop out, already sweating frantically, and opened up the feed that showed me Grizzy's living room. I pushed back from my desk.

My best friend was tied up on the living room floor, eyes pleading, and a cloth tied over her mouth.

Fourteen

Pepper spray wasn't enough to deal with this situation. I had no idea who was in there, but calling the cops might end my best friend's life. And what about Oliver? I needed a darn gun, and I was going to get one when this was through. If Special Agent Roberts didn't like it, she could eat rocks.

I'd left Aggy at the office with strict instructions not to follow me or tell anyone that I'd left. Mindy wouldn't breathe a word, mostly because she'd barely noticed me walking out the front door.

I hid behind a tree, surveying the house for any signs of disturbance. The roof was free of gunmen. The yard was quiet, the flowerbeds untouched, and the street was empty of suspicious vehicles, but that didn't mean anything.

Curly Fries, interestingly, was in the living room

window, glaring out at the world through grumpy, narrowed yellow eyes.

That's not right.

If Grizzy was in danger, Curly Fries would either be nowhere in sight or behaving like a wild animal. Curly hated everyone except for Griselda and Oliver. She would never have sat idly by.

Regardless, the camera had shown me what was going on. Grizzy needed help.

How was I going to approach this? I could sneak through the back or—

The door was open ajar. It creaked, drifting inward, and my suspicions doubled. What the heck was going on around here? A trap? It had to be.

But I couldn't risk Grizzy and Oliver, trap or not.

I brought out my pepper spray and strode toward the porch. The creak of hinges sent a thrill down my spine. Nobody appeared in the doorway. I crept toward it, up Grizzy's stepping stone path and onto the familiar porch.

This place was my home too, and the thought that it had been invaded enraged me.

I took a breath and calmed myself—the last thing I wanted was to mess this up by being too emotional. I checked the feed on my phone.

Grizzy was on the floor, her eyes closed, but no one

else was in sight. The living room was entirely clear, unless an attacker was waiting behind the sofa.

My gut said they would be guarding behind the door and in the kitchen. Anywhere the camera wasn't pointing. They had either found it or had positioned themselves at ingress points where it would be easiest to attack me.

Now.

I kicked the door all the way open and it collided with something.

A muffled feminine cry rang out.

The Somerville Spiders had sent a woman. I brought the spray up and a second attacker leaped out of the kitchen doorway with both hands up. I brought my finger down on the button atop the pepper spray, but stopped myself in the nick of time.

Because that second attacker wore a floral apron and held a wooden spoon aloft, the end covered in cookie dough. A big blob of said cookie dough dropped off and onto the living room carpeting.

"Sorry, Griselda," Vee said, pulling a face.

Mississippi appeared from behind the door, rubbing her nose. "That's going to leave a bruise, Watson."

Grizzy sighed. She sat upright and had the gag she'd been wearing a moment ago in her hand. Not tied up.

"Are you crazy?" I thundered at the twins. "What the heck do you think you're doing? I could have pepper-sprayed you in the face. I could have killed you! I thought you were—" I cut off.

"Yes?" Mississippi asked, circling a hand in front of me to encourage me to keep talking.

Vee came forward and took me by the arm, drawing me inside.

Missi shut the door and locked it.

"Where's Oliver?" I asked, still in attack-mode. A part of me was sure that the Spiders were in the house.

"He's napping upstairs," Grizzy said, rising from the floor. "You got here quick. Thanks. I was worried I'd have to lie on the floor with Arthur's tie in my mouth for hours." She lifted it and smiled at me. It was covered in polka dots.

I ground my teeth.

I'd been right. This was a trap, just not the type of trap I'd anticipated.

Missi plopped down on Grizzy's comfy leather sofa. Vee cleaned up the cookie dough then grabbed a mixing bowl from the kitchen and stood there, mixing away like this was a regular day. Grizzy gestured to an armchair, standing in the middle of the living room.

"It's time, Chris," she said. "Come on."

"I don't know what you're talking about," I said.

"We know you've been bugging our homes." Grizzy's tone was warm and kind. "And I told the twins you'd never do anything to violate our privacy unless you thought it was absolutely necessary, so how about you tell us what's going on?"

"If we're in danger," Missi said, "we have the right to know."

"She's right, dear."

"Of course, I'm right." Missi flapped her hands in the air and let them fall into her lap. "When am I ever wrong?"

"I'm barely finished baking the cookies. You can't give me impossible tasks so soon after—"

"Oh ho, very funny," Missi snapped. "Anyway, what is it, Watson? What's going on?"

"I can't tell you."

"But you can," Vee replied.

"And you will." Missi folded her arms.

"Don't you trust us by now, Chris?" Grizzy asked, shaking her head. "How many years has it been? How many murders and mysteries and gosh... We've been through it with you."

"I was told—"

"Since when do you do what you're told?" Missi asked.

"Fine," I said, walking to the proffered armchair and throwing myself into it. I covered my face with a hand. "Fine. I don't care what I'm told to do, you're right, but I do care what you three think of me. I can't stand the guilt and the shame of endangering the people I care about, and

94

that's exactly what's going on. I've put your lives in danger again."

"How?" Missi asked, but her voice wasn't unkind.

I held back tears.

"Is it them?" Grizzy asked. "Are they back?" She'd been through it with me. She'd nearly died because of my investigation into my mother's cold case, years ago.

I lifted my gaze to meet hers. "The Somerville Spiders are back."

Missi and Vee exchanged worried glances.

"I thought I disbanded them, or, our investigation and actions disbanded them, but I was wrong. An FBI agent came by and warned me about them. She gave me strict instructions not to tell anyone except for Liam and Aggy."

"That girl's been acting different lately," Missi said. "Didn't I say that, Vee? Didn't I?"

"Different is Agatha's middle name," Vee replied. "How could you possibly tell?"

But the women quieted after that statement, the three of them lost in thoughts, their brows wrinkling.

"That settles it then," Missi said. "We're all getting guns."

"What?" Grizzy said. "I can't have a gun. I don't know how to shoot a gun. We—"

"We'll teach you," Vee replied. "Or Missi will. She's the better shooter between the two of us."

Grizzy's expression lightened. "Oh," she said. "Sounds fun."

"Yes," Vee said. "But I have to finish these cookies first." And then she bustled toward the kitchen.

"I should check on Oliver." Grizzy rose.

"But—" I opened my mouth to apologize to them, but each of my friends gave me a look in turn. A smile, a shake of the head, and in Missi's case, a rolling of her eyes. There was no need to apologize.

I covered my face again, weeping. This time, Missi, Vee, and Griselda gathered around me to give me a hug.

Fifteen

That evening...

My friends were superheroes for accepting what I'd told them. I was beyond lucky. And I was also determined to keep them safe, and to keep Sleepy Creek free of murder and the Somerville Spiders.

After an early dinner with Aggy and Liam, we'd wiped the pizza grease off our hands, and I'd driven Agatha over to Missi and Vee's place. They were having a movie night, while I was determined to do reconnaissance at Mr. Sinclair's practice.

I parked the Corvette around the corner from First Street and got out into the night, cursing how hot it was as

I snapped a pair of latex gloves onto my hands. If I pulled off what I had planned, then I'd need them, but I was already covered in sweat.

Get it together, Watson. I strode down the street, tucking my hands into the pockets of my shorts so as to hide the gloves from sight from potential passersby.

But the street was empty.

Light from the lampposts cast vignettes on the paved sidewalks. The buildings in first street were squat, single stories, a few of them with flower beds outfront, while others had paved parking areas.

Gordon Sinclair's practice, a white building with his name painted across the front in curling letters, had a breezeway that led around the side of the building along the border wall. I glanced left and right, checking for Spiders or random people who might be lurking in the shadows, and then strode onto the property.

I hopped a wall that bisected the breezeway and landed at the back of the practice, which had a grassy yard and an old oak, its gnarled roots lifting the wall behind it.

A back porch held an old swing seat. The lights were off inside, but I'd expected that—working hours were over, and Mr. Sinclair didn't strike me as the type of person who worked overtime.

I checked the window closest to the back door and found it was locked, but the latch holding that lock in place was ancient. I grabbed a twig from under the oak tree then returned to the window, pulled on it and jimmied the twig through the gap, lifting the latch with ease.

"Gotcha," I muttered.

I climbed into Mr. Sinclair's comfy office.

I left the window open in case I needed a hasty escape and switched on my flashlight, casting the beam around.

A leather chaise lounge was positioned beneath the window, an impressive desk spanned the wall to my left, and the rest of the room was tastefully decorated with a bookshelf, laden with thick-spined books, and a filing cabinet in the corner.

That oversized desk—Mr. Sinclair had matched it to the size of his ego—had three drawers on each side. I opened them and rifled through the contents. Sweet wrappers, an unused notepad, a clipboard, a couple of discarded pens, and a key.

I lifted it out and examined it. *Looks like the key to a filing cabinet.*

But was I really going to snoop through Mr. Sinclair's private files? He'd delivered information to Mona Jonah in a brown folder—where were those?

Despite my doubts, I used the key to unlock the filing cabinet.

I slid the gray top drawer open and began rifling through the files. I wasn't going to touch anything that didn't pertain to the case. But it felt awful, going through names of private clients. It was like going to a hospital and reading other people's charts. It didn't sit right with me, but I had to mince the meat to make the hamburger patty.

Gordon was suspicious. He was feeding Mona information, but what type of information was it and where could I find it?

I used the flashlight to illuminate the tabs, bearing names, on the folders and my fingers stalled.

ELODIE KING.

The victim had been Gordon Sinclair's patient.

You can't seriously pry.

But I wouldn't get this information from Gordon himself, and the cops weren't working with me either. I needed a win, and this would have to be it.

If Elodie King had been here, talking to Gordon, there might be something in this file that led me to the killer. Gordon had been Elodie's therapist and was potentially exposing his patients to Mona. That or there was some other exchange of information going on that was unconnected to his practice.

I placed it on the desk and opened the folder.

I paged through several typed and handwritten notes, skimming their contents.

July 20th

Elodie is convinced that her brother is after her. Paranoid delusions? More assessment required. She claims that Noel is constantly stalking and harassing her, though she won't reveal the reason as to why to me. When asked why she doesn't report these instances to the police, Elodie insists that the police won't help her and they're in on it. This could be further evidence that her anxiety and obsessive compulsive disorder are progressing, but again, further analysis required.

I'm considering recommending Elodie see a psychiatrist in Logan's Rest due to these disturbances. Talk therapy and even Cognitive Behavioral Therapy have yielded little results.

Elodie believes that dwelling on the traumas and deep internal wounds that are bothering her will only draw further attention to them and make her condition worse.

July 25th

Elodie had a nervous breakdown in my office this morning. Thankfully, I was able to calm her. She has an upcoming performance which has been the cause of a lot of added stress, due to a fear of performing. That is my assumption, as she will not tell me why she fears this particular performance.

She's mentioned several times that her brother is after

her wealth and that Simone, her friend, broke up with him because of it.

I've referred her to Dr. Ivan Schwarz in Logan's Rest and will be closing her file.

And it was the last entry.

I paged back through it until I found her general patient information.

NAME: Elodie King
INITIAL COMPLAINT: Suffering from generalized anxiety and phobias related to familial trauma.
EMERGENCY CONTACT: Simone Ellsworth.
PRE-EXISTING HEALTH CONDITIONS: Chronic fatigue. Previous depressive episodes. Hospitalized for a frac-tured skull.

A fractured skull? How had that happened? Already, I had more information about the victim than I'd garnered in the past couple of evenings, scouring the internet. I took pictures of the pages with my phone, in case I needed to peruse them later, then carefully returned everything to the folder and then to the filing cabinet.

I left the office exactly as I'd found it, closing the window behind me and using the stick to bring the latch back down into place.

And then I was out of there, stripping off the gloves as I went. Gordon Sinclair had a finger in every pie in this town, and Elodie had been afraid of Noel, who had denied knowing her, let alone being her brother.

I had my next lead.

Sixteen

The following morning...

I SIPPED MY COFFEE IN MY CORVETTE, MY EYES narrowed at the new car dealership. King's Motors was flashy with a red inflatable tube man out front, his arms waggling excitedly in the morning sunlight. Cars were parked in the lot in front of the white building, with its glass windows that looked in on yet more cars. Specials and exciting sale prices were plastered in windscreens, and salesmen flittered around, talking to anyone who dared step through the gates.

"Are you getting a new car?" Aggy asked, from the passenger seat.

"Definitely not." I loved my Corvette. It had given out a couple of times and I'd had to get it fixed, repeatedly, but I wasn't selling this baby any time soon. Not until I had a child of my own.

The thought made my palms sweat, so I pushed it to the side. Liam and I could barely manage our businesses and Agatha, let alone a child. Thank goodness my cat, Poirot, was such an unmitigated delight. He was too intelligent to make a mess of the toilet paper or spray our furniture, though he did get a mean case of the zoomies at three in the morning.

"Then we're here for Mr. King," Agatha said, adjusting her fedora. "Just as I accepted."

"You mean, as you 'suspected.'"

"No. I accepted that we were coming here to interview Mr. King."

I was too tired to argue with her. I'd stayed up late last night poring over the clues and the information from Gordon Sinclair's folder on Elodie. I hadn't bothered searching for Simone's folder while I'd been in there—it felt risky to go through it, unethical even. But Elodie's folder had presented a risk I was willing to take. She had passed on. Didn't that technically mean the client-therapist relationship was over?

I was rationalizing the bad thing that I'd done, though I couldn't bring myself to regret it. Because doing the bad thing had brought me directly to Noel King's place of work.

"You want to wait in the car?" I asked.

"Christie, it's boiling," Aggy said.

"I'll crack a window for you."

She gave me a mutinous glare. My mannerisms were rubbing off on her—more trouble for me.

"Come on." We got out of the car and walked toward King's Motors. We walked past that inflatable tube man, eternally trapped in a state of falsified joy, doomed to watch on as people drove away in their pre-owned cars, living a life of freedom of which he could only dream and—

"Welcome to King's Motors," a man said, with a jaunty wobble of his head. "Name's Patrick and I'm honored to be of service to you today. Every woman deserves a King motor."

Aggy had stopped a pace back to stare at the giant red waving arms of the inflatable tube man.

"Nice to meet you," I said, sticking out a hand. "Christie Watson."

"That your old beater over there?" Patrick asked, pointing to my beloved Corvette.

"Sure." I'd figured the best way to get to Noel King was to play the part. Calling and talking to him hadn't worked, and if he caught wind of who I was, he wouldn't let anything slip. Let him believe I was just another sucker here for a pre-owned car and a free tank of gas. One with every sale, according to the billboard.

"I take it you're looking for something sporty," Patrick said, removing a comb from the inside pocket of his jacket and sweeping it through his glistening black hair. He had to be broiling in that suit. Poor man was as pink as a pork chop.

"Maybe," I said. "I'm open to change."

"But I thought we weren't getting a new car," Aggy said. "I thought we were going to talk to—"

I stepped on my cousin's toe, and she yelped. "Careful, Aggy." And stopped her from tripping. She got the picture and didn't say anything more.

"Patrick Dalton." He stuck out his hand to Agatha and performed an exaggerated bow, wriggling his eyebrows at her. "And may I say that your fedora is very fetching."

Aggy blushed as pink as he was. A pair of pork chops sizzling in the summer's heat. "All right," I said, and took my cousin's hand from his before Patrick managed to plant a kiss on her unsuspecting fingers. "We came for a car, not for... Whatever this is."

Patrick, appropriately cowed, led the way through the lot.

"I kind of liked it," Aggy whispered.

I gasped. I never gasped. "What do you mean you liked it?"

"He's cute," Aggy said.

"Agatha," I breathed. "He is a car salesman."

"And so? I'm a nobody. I don't even have a real job or a bakery. Who am I to judge him for what he does?"

"That's not the point," I said. "He's..." But she was right. He came off greasy, but that didn't mean he was greasy. But my cousin Aggy deserved the best. "Anyway, don't talk about yourself like that." My tone was firm. "You're one in a billion."

"I am?" She fluttered her eyelashes at me, her fedora skew a top her red bob.

"One in two billion," I corrected.

Patrick, who'd been walking ahead of us the entire time, stopped in a section of convertible cars. "I think we'll be able to find something you'll like here," he said, then patted the hood of the car closest to him. "This beauty has been waiting for—"

"What about those?" I pointed to the cars that were closest to the front of the building.

"The four-seaters?" Patrick sounded momentarily confused. "Uh, sure! We've got a couple of Volvos that have your name on them."

"Hope not. That would be creepy."

Patrick guffawed like I'd made the funniest joke he'd ever heard.

Aggy fell into step beside me. "Keep him busy, will you?" I whispered.

She blushed again, but immediately fell back to start a conversation with the car salesman. Patrick cleared his throat multiple times, reaching up and adjusting his collared shirt as they talked. I had to admit, he wasn't a bad looking guy. He wasn't good enough for my cousin.

Nobody was good enough for my cousin.

I hovered near the cars, pretending to be interested in them while I studied the interior of the building through those glistening windows.

Noel King strode between the vehicles, talking on the phone. His chest was puffed out, and I could almost hear his booming voice just by watching him. He stopped beside a car, shaking his head, then beckoned to someone out of sight.

Simone strode into view. Her arms were folded as she walked toward him, her chin tilted upward. She stopped about a pace away from Mr. King, and the argument began. Simone tapped him on the chest with the back of her hand.

Noel laughed heartily at the gesture and patted her on the shoulder, tilting his head to the side.

Whatever he'd said, she raised a palm, but she never let

the slap fly. Instead, she stormed out of the building and through the lot, past me and toward the open gates.

Simone and Noel were connected too. They had been "ex-lovers" according to Elodie's file. But was it true?

Seventeen

"You're going to stay in the car," I said, directing the Corvette past the Burger Bar. We were headed to the wealthier side of town. Back when I'd first arrived a few of the Sleepy Creekers had called it "Money Bags Town", but the name had never stuck.

"But, Christie," Aggy started, her tone whining.

"No," I said. "I can't do this if you're with me, but we have to act fast. I need you to listen to me, Agatha. I wouldn't ask you for this if it wasn't entirely necessary."

Aggy let out a sigh, shaking her head and folding her arms. "You could drop me off at the Burger Bar."

"We've already passed it," I said, and took the turn off.

When Mr. Noel King had arrived in Sleepy Creek and set up that car dealership, the news had rippled through the town. The same wasn't true for Elodie. She had arrived in silence and then created beautiful music.

Noel had a reputation. The rich bachelor who lived in a mansion in the richest suburb of town, right on Downtown Street. It was ironic since the mansions, situated on a long stretch of road shaded by trees, was uptown.

Aggy rolled down her window in a sulk, and I let her.

Mr. King was otherwise engaged, and that gave me the opportunity to scope out his house for clues. I doubted I'd be able to get inside during the day, but there would be *something* I could find—that was the hope.

The mansion was near the end of that long street, and its gates were open. A pick up truck was parked in front of the grand staircase that led to a porch and a triple story home, the front of which was made entirely of windows.

"A glass house," I said. "More irony."

Aggy sniffed.

The pick-up outside bore the logo for Creek Construction. "And it looks like there's construction going on, which gives us easy access."

Aggy clicked her tongue.

"Aggy," I said. "I have a job for you."

She perked up instantly, pushing her fedora off to the left of her head.

"Call Simone Ellsworth for me and see if you can ascertain her alibi," I said.

Aggy fiddled with her seatbelt. "Are you sure?" She hadn't been the best at interpersonal relationships or questioning the suspects, but I could relate to that.

"I'm sure," I said. "I'll expect results when I get back to the car." And then I got out and shut the door, tucking my hands into the pockets of my shorts and strolling up the cobblestone drive that led past a lawn that needed watering.

I didn't have high hopes for Aggy getting results, not because of her unique personality, but because Simone had been evasive when we talked, and she would barely remember Agatha. Besides Simone, the rest of the suspects in the case weren't willing to talk to me, and that was frustrating. How was I meant to establish a timeline and their alibis? Asking around would bring Detective Hardwick down on my head, and I preferred not being involved with him.

The sounds of a saw and hammering penetrated the mansion, and workers moved in and out of the front rooms, obvious through the windows. It was quite literally a glass house. Either Noel didn't value his privacy or he enjoyed the thought of others watching him. Arrogance? It suited his personality.

I started up the steps, but a man exited the house and stopped me with a whistle and a hand up. He wore a construction helmet and a navy blue shirt that was faded from hard work under the sun. The logo "Creek Construction" was embroidered on the breast pocket.

"I help you, Miss?"

"Miss Desiree Darling,"I said, with a purr in my voice. I extended a hand. "Apologies, I was waiting for my real estate agent to arrive."

"Heh?" The guy shifted his hard hat. "Look, lady, this is private property and we're working on the house. It's not safe here. Now—"

"I'm here for a tour," I said, doing my best impression of an imperious rich woman. "I'm considering buying the property."

"We weren't told about, uh, any tour," the guy said.

"And you're always privy to what the home owner does?" I checked my nails. "It's fine. I'll wait out here. My agent will be here shortly."

The guy shrugged at me and muttered about this being beyond his paygrade before entering the mansion. I didn't have to go in, it turned out. Just walk around the exterior of the building, given that I could see inside.

I kept my hands tucked in my pockets and took a leisurely stroll along the wraparound porch, pretending to study the interior with "rich people disapproval." It was difficult to keep the awe off my face.

Noel King had taste, I'd give him that. No wonder he wanted the floor-to-ceiling windows. His house was tastefully decorated, not too sparse, with antiques and rugs, vases and beautiful art sculptures. I circled the house, stopping to admire the rooms I passed, until I happened upon the study.

The construction workers weren't in here, but the curtains were drawn back to show off a large walnut desk, a gun safe, and a rifle.

The rifle hung on the wall behind the desk. It had a scope. It was clearly a hunting rifle, given the stuffed heads of animals mounted nearby, and it was potentially a match for the murder weapon.

Could be an antique. Doesn't necessarily have to be a working hunting rifle.

But I brought out my phone and snapped a picture of it.

Noel had been dating Simone, he'd denied knowing his own sister, and I'd witnessed him arguing with her. And he was a good shooter with a rifle that might be a match for the murder weapon. I wouldn't be able to tell until that information was released.

A text blipped through on my phone, and I affected the bored lean of a woman who had too much time and money on her hands, just in case a construction worker or foreman decided to check what I was up to.

She wouldn't tell me anything.

That's all right. I'm sure you did your best.

Do you want me to talk to the other suspects? Gordon and the King?

Let's not name him the King. You can call him if you want.

Call him? But I can just talk to him now.

Huh?

He's coming up the driveway in his fancy black car.

Aggy, that's really information I could have used two minutes ago.

The front of the mansion was too far away for me to hear the arrival of the car. I forced myself to breathe. Panicking wouldn't get me anywhere, but I turned left and right, doing exactly that, and searching for an escape.

I could dive off the side of the wraparound porch, but there were rose bushes down there that looked killer. Before I could make the decision, a figure appeared in the doorway to the study.

Noel King strode inside, phone in hand, his attention on it rather than his surroundings. Lucky. I backed out of sight, pressing against the window of the room next door, but tilting my head so I could spy on him through a crack in the curtains.

Eighteen

NOEL GAVE A MUFFLED SIGH AND SAT DOWN IN the leather executive chair at his desk, tapping away on his phone.

A knock came at his study door, and he pulled a face, turning as the construction worker who had stopped me from entering the house strode in.

Time to run.

"Sir," he said. "Do you mind if I—?"

"Not right now, Jeff," he said. "I'm in the middle of something important."

"But I—"

"I have a phone call to make. Talk to me later." Noel rose from his seat and walked the man out of the room, bearing down on him, that dark beard particularly grizzly this morning.

Jeff scrambled out of the study, though he looked as if he still wanted to interrupt. My guess was that he'd wanted to tell Mr. King about the presence of the crazy woman who claimed to be waiting for a real estate agent on his property.

Saved by the, uh, phone?

King shut his study door in the man's face and walked back to the desk, scowling. A moment later, his phone rang and he answered it. "Mother," he said.

I raised an eyebrow. Noel's parents were alive. Why weren't they in Sleepy Creek, mourning the death of their daughter or seeking out justice?

"Yes, I've been talking to the authorities," Noel said, irritably. "They've advised me to keep my opinions about the case to myself."

A pause.

"No, I don't think that will be necessary. If you and Father come here, it will draw more attention to our family that we don't need. I've just set up the business. It's not my problem that she refused to listen to us."

That had to be Elodie he was complaining about.

"Yeah, but if we do that, it's going to make me look suspicious, and I've already got strangers asking questions and insinuating that I was involved. I don't want— No. I didn't do that. That is *not* the reason I moved here. Maybe if you would listen, I— Yeah, I understand that." Noel grabbed his forehead, resting his elbow atop the desk. "I have done everything you wanted me to do. Everything. What more could there be?"

Tension in the family. That could have affected the bond between siblings.

"I did that!" Noel's deep, rumbling voice had taken on a pitched tone that was verging on desperate. "I did everything you asked of me. She wouldn't listen. What else was I supposed to do?" A breath. "You can't blame me for this. Do you think I wanted this to happen? I would never have — No." He dropped his hand to the desk with a thud. "No, Mother. No. Yeah. I won't let anything— You can't be serious. I don't want to host a memorial service for her. You basically wrote her off and now I—"

There was a long period of silence from Noel, at least a minute, as he listened to his Mother talking on the other end of the phone. I couldn't hear her words or her tone due to the glass, but his expression grew darker with the passing seconds.

"Goodbye, Mother." He tore the phone away from his ear and let out a furious roar.

Noel cocked his hand back and threw the phone at the wall to his left. It shattered into pieces and thudded to the fancy carpeting. Mr. King, usually wearing fake smiles, stood in his study, breathing like a winded rhinoceros. He brought himself back to calm slowly, then squared his shoulders and rearranged things on his desk, though they were already neatly placed.

A knock came moments later.

"Come in," Noel said, quietly.

Jeff, the construction worker, entered. "Sorry to interrupt, Mr. King, but we believe there's an intruder on the property."

And that's my cue.

I pushed off from the glass and walked along the wraparound porch, swiftly. I didn't break into a run just yet—it would seem suspicious as I strode past those vast windows looking in on rooms filled with construction workers.

I didn't glance into them this time, though I sensed their gazes following me.

I reached the corner and peeked around it. Coast was clear for now. I strode down the steps and reached the cobblestone walk. Inside the mansion, someone gave a shout. I sprinted down the driveway, colliding with the side of the Corvette when I reached it.

Aggy was on the edge of her seat inside. I ripped my door open and leaped into the car.

The car started first try, and I spcd off, just as Jeff ran out onto the porch.

"Wahoo!" Aggy let out a cry as we took a corner at high speed.

I checked my rearview mirror repeatedly, hoping that

Noel wouldn't have the wherewithal to jump into a vehicle of his own and follow me.

"That was cool."

"Next time a suspect arrives at a place I'm investigating, let me know right away."

"Sure. I didn't think it was that big of a deal," Aggy replied. "it seemed like you wanted to run into him."

I didn't give the idea credence. Instead, I drove us back to Liam's house, rather than the apartment. I needed a cup of coffee from home and to ground myself and think about what I'd discovered.

Noel King didn't want to draw the attention of the cops. He was being pressured by his parents, and he had insinuated that they weren't happy with Elodie's actions. But what had Elodie done to upset them? And did this mean that they were suspects themselves?

Where did they live?

Simone and Noel were connected.

I parked the car in the garage, just in case King was on the look out for my Corvette. I doubted that was the case, but it was better to be safe than have an angry murder suspect on my doorstep.

Aggy followed me inside, and Poirot greeted me at the door.

I bent and picked him up, pressing a kiss to his fore-

THE CHEESE BURGER MURDER

head. Poirot gave me a lick on the chin, signaling his undying appreciation for the affection. He was a very proper cat, the two black circles around his eyes had always made him look the part of a bespectacled gentleman, as had the dark strokes below his snout that gave the illusion of a mustache.

I set Poirot down on the table and went over to the coffee pot in the corner, lost in thought.

"What happened, Christie?" Aggy asked.

"Noel King is either the murderer or he had something to gain from Elodie's death and this was a happy coincidence for him," I said. "He's not unhappy that his sister is dead. He seems pleased that she's out of the picture and annoyed that he has to deal with this at all."

I told my cousin about the call with his parents, partly because Aggy often saw connections I didn't because of how her mind worked, and because I needed to hear myself repeat it out loud.

"I have to find out more about the King family. Let's grab a bite from the Burger Bar after this and then we'll do research. I'm sure the twins would be willing to help."

Aggy smiled.

"We'll have to walk into the town though."

Her face fell.

"Come on, Agatha, exercise is good for the soul." As

was solving murder cases, but a creeping itch at the back of my neck told me that the Somerville Spiders were a problem, and that they weren't going away soon. The longer I remained distracted the more dangerous they became.

Nineteen

Missi and Vee were at their usual table in the Burger Bar, both sipping double thick chocolate milk-shakes, their heads bent together over something on the table. They weren't the only ones—the tables were full in the diner, the customers gossiping and reading copies of Mona's new gossip rag.

I sat down beside Missi and Aggy took a place next to Vee.

"I thought she wasn't publishing another pamphlet for a month," I said, and waved down Hedy.

The dark-haired, pretty server swept over, giving us a quick albeit frazzled smile. She had to be spinning in here thanks to how busy it was. She wasn't working alone, as Martin, Grizzy's second-in-command, had thrown on an apron to help.

"Two Cheese Burger specials, fries, and chocolate shakes please." Aggy and I always ate the special of the week.

"Coming right up," Hedy said, and hurried off to put in our orders. Jarvis, the chef, pinged the bell repeatedly—burger specials were ferried past our table repeatedly, as folks needed their appetites sated while they consumed juicy gossip.

"What's the news?" I asked.

Missi sipped her milkshake, an eye twitching.

"Did she mention your antique store?" Aggy asked.

I held my breath, but Vee shook her head. "Not this time," she replied.

"But she will," Missi said. "She will. If I know anything about Mona Jonah it's that she can't resist a fight, and after we shouted at her the other day, there's no way she won't take the bait and publish lies about us."

"She's focusing on the murder," Vee said.

"We think that it's because of that nephew of hers. Detective Hardwick." Missi drew her straw through her milkshake. "He's obviously struggling to figure out what happened and she's trying to flush out more gossip."

"May I read it?" I asked.

Vee slid the pamphlet over to me.

DISASTER REIGNS IN SLEEPY CREEK! VIOLINIST MURDERED AT PEACEFUL CONCERT!

It's come to my attention that there's been talk about the death of Miss Elodie King, violinist, who was brutally murdered earlier this week. As a result, I've decided to publish a second gossip pamphlet, to sate the rumor mill.

As a well-connected individual in Sleepy Creek, you can trust that what I have to say is true. I, Mona Jonah, the Queen of Gossip in Sleepy Creek and—

"I can't believe she's allowed to publish this stuff," I muttered. "It's so badly written."

"Thank you!" Missi threw up her hands.

—your chief deliverer of gossip have come to the conclusion that I have to take matters into my own hands and deliver this truth directly to you, my dear gossiper.

Elodie King is none other than the relative, the sister, of Mr. Noel King, the most eligible bachelor in town, who happens to be fabulously wealthy But here's the interesting thing, she wasn't rich like her brother. In fact, she was totally BROKE.

PENNILESS. That should have been her middle name. Because she had no money when she died.

"So bad," I muttered.

Hedy delivered our milkshakes and burgers, and I ate my fries idly while I skimmed the pamphlet for relevant clues or leads. Anything that wasn't Mona self-aggrandizing.

—wouldn't you know it? Noel King used to be involved with local wedding planner, Simone Ellsworth. According to my documentation, the pair were dating some time in the past, but had broken up due to a disagreement.

But that told me nothing new, except that my suspicions about Gordon Sinclair were correct. He had definitely shared confidential information with Mona. But what did he stand to gain by giving her that information, what was she providing him in turn?

Sinclair wouldn't offer up private information, that could land him in a lot of legal trouble, without standing to gain a prize that was equal to what he was offering up.

Was he trying to throw people off his trail? He was a shooter, just like Simone and Noel, which made him a potential suspect, and he was connected to Elodie. He had been her therapist. And what about the accusation that Noel had been a stalker?

The way he'd acted during that phone call today had been threatening. That fit the bill of a stalker or a man who desperately wanted control over the situation. But then, anger didn't make a person bad, only human.

I slid the pamphlet back over to Vee, frowning. "It's awfully written."

"But people will buy it," Vee sighed, tucking the pamphlet into her bag and bringing out her iPad.

"We should start our own website," Missi said, suddenly. "Debunking everything the Gossip Circle and Mona put out."

"And start a range war?" Vee asked, tapping away on her iPad screen. "Doesn't seem wise."

"We can't let her walk all over us," Missi hissed. "Or this town."

I ate a fry and scanned the diner. The locals were enjoying themselves, eating their burgers and reading the atrocious pamphlet. I had to admit it, Sleepy Creekers loved their gossip. Mona knew what her target audience liked.

"I need information," I said.

Vee's sharp blue eyes met mine. "Go on, dear." Missi and Vee had always been my eyes and ears in town. Unlike Mona, they were discreet when it came to handling and dealing out gossip. They didn't create or spread rumors, but dropped clues when I needed them.

"I want to know everything about the King family."

And then I told my friends about what I'd witnessed at the King residence.

Missi slapped the table afterward. "Knew it. That dealership is too good to be true, and Mona's been so far up that Noel guy's butt, he can probably taste her cheap perfume in the back of his throat."

"Mississippi!" Vee was stern. "That is vile."

"Sorry." Missi had the good manners to look cowed after her sister's dressing down.

Vee turned to me while Aggy inhaled her burger, eating loud enough that the woman at the booth behind her turned around with a disgusted expression.

"I'll find what I can and forward it to you, Christie," Vee said. "It shouldn't take long."

"She's a professional," Missi said. "Seriously, I don't know how she does it. I've never been that good with the internet, not compared to her."

"Thank you," I said. "I owe you one."

"One?"

"Fine. I owe you a lot." Especially after the "bugged apartment" incident. "Have you guys seen Grizzy?"

"She hasn't been around this morning," Vee said.

My pulse raced, but Missi laid a hand on my forearm. "Relax. She's taking the morning off. We stopped by her house to check on her first thing. Have you heard back from your busking friend?"

I'd told the twins and Griselda about Special Agent Roberts and her disguise as Sapphire Blaze. I shook my head. "No," I said. "And it's stressing me out."

"Don't worry, Watson," Missi said. "We'll get through this together."

Vee gave me a bright smile. "We're family."

And that was exactly what worried me. Family was dangerous. I'd learned that when the Somerville Spiders had taken my mother from me.

Twenty

That afternoon...

AT FIVE IN THE AFTERNOON, I OPENED MY SILVER laptop—purchased with the proceeds from my private investigation business—and leaned back in my creaky chair, rocking back and forth as I considered what Vee had sent me.

She'd been lightning quick with her research, and had discovered that an old friend from New York ran in the same circles as the King family.

Christie,

I hope this helps. See the email I received from Alberta below.

–

Hi Vee,

Oh gosh, it's so wonderful to hear from you. Funny how life works—I was just thinking to myself the other day, I wonder how Virginia and Mississippi are doing? And then I received your email today!

The kids are doing well, thank you very much, and the grandbabies are a delight. I get to see them every weekend. How are things in that chaotic little town of yours? Still crazy as a bag full of fleas?

As for your query about the King family, there's a lot I could tell you. None of it is very nice.

The Kings are a highly influential and wealthy family in New York. I've known the matriarch, Ursuline, for years, though we've never really seen eye-to-eye, if you know what I mean. She's a rigid human being. Likes things done her way and if she doesn't get them, she's liable to throw a fit. And her husband is a pushover. Lets her do whatever she wants.

There were rumors floating around about them—that they had an iron-grip over their children's lives, for instance, and often threatened to remove their inheritance if they didn't follow the right path. Elodie, their youngest, is the black sheep of the family, while Noel is the golden child. Always doing mommy and daddy's bidding.

I'm coming off mean, but they've got a reputation, and I've had my fair share of run-ins with the mother. She's never been kind or welcoming, and she's gone out of her way to spread rumors about me. Everyone avoids the Kings.

I heard that the son, Noel, had moved out of state. Is he close to you?

Anyway, email me back with your news! So lovely to hear from you!

Love,

Alberta

That made sense. Elodie was penniless, according to Mona's gossip column, and if that was true, it was because her parents had disowned her. But why?

It explained why they hadn't arrived in Sleepy Creek demanding answers like a normal parent would have done in this situation.

"Christie?" Aggy piped up, from her stool in the corner. "When can we get dinner?"

"You're not full from the Cheese Burger special?" I asked. "I'm stuffed."

"I was hoping we could meet Liam at Slice of Nice for a pizza."

I couldn't stomach a pizza, but a walk through town and a visit to my fiancé sure sounded nice. "We can do that. Just give me a minute to—"

My office door bounced open and hit the wall, and Investigator Brown skulked in, glaring at me. This was the second time in the span of a week. Shoot, I had to beef up security around here. Pepper spray wasn't enough. Missi had mentioned getting guns, and I was on board with the idea.

"Watson," Brown said, striding toward my desk. "I've been looking for you everywhere."

"Once again, your powers of deduction and investigation prove lacking," I said. "We've been here for hours. You can't have looked *everywhere.*"

Brown chewed on air.

Aggy sniggered.

"What do you want, Brown?" I asked. "I was about to close for the day. Let me guess, you need my help solving your case. Well, if that's the case, it'll cost you."

"How dare you!" Brown fiddled with the tie on his trench coat. He insisted on dressing like an old-timey private investigator from back in the day. "I don't need your help. I'm the one the police came to for help in the first place."

I grabbed my cellphone from my purse. "We'll see about that," I said.

"What are you doing?" he asked.

"Nothing."

> Hey, Arthur. How are things going with Brown?

I hadn't asked Arthur about the investigation because I didn't want to put him in an awkward position. He was my fiancé's best friend and my best friend's husband, as well as the father to my godchild. I wasn't about to mess that up.

> He's a fool, but Hardwick insists that we rely on him for extra evidence, whatever that means. I think he's one of Mona's stooges, honestly. It's dumb that we have to rely on anyone when we have two detectives working this case.

> Sounds like a pain.

> Working with Hardwick has been a lesson in patience. I shouldn't say more. It's unprofessional.

"Who are you talking to?" Brown slapped his hand down on my desk, and I considered it.

"You looking to lose fingers?" I asked.

Brown retracted the hand and cleared his throat.

"Look, Watson, I didn't come here for a fight," he said. "I —I'm sorry. I lost my temper the other day."

"And now," Aggy said.

Brown gritted his teeth. "And now."

"What do you want, Brown?"

He wet his thin, dry little lips. "I want what you've got on the case."

Ah. He wanted my help, he just wanted to find fun ways to phrase it because he had an over-sized ego to match that trench coat. "And what are you going to give me in return?" I asked. "Maybe we can broker a deal here, Brown. A win-win situation."

Aggy shook her head frantically in the background, but she didn't need to worry. I didn't trust this guy either.

"Fine," Brown said, and sat his oversized hawkish person in the chair in front of my desk. "What do you want to know?"

"Does Simone Ellsworth have an alibi for the time of the murder."

Brown's eyes widened. "You think she's a suspect, eh?" He laughed. "Maybe you can't help me."

"I'll take that as a yes."

"She has an alibi, yes," he said. "She was with a friend that night."

"Was the friend Gordon Sinclair?" I asked.

Brown's laugh sounded like a sneeze. "Wouldn't you

like to know? Give me something. Give me what you have."

"What I have is a growing disdain for you, Brown," I replied. "I don't see why it's necessary to keep things from me when you were the one who came in here cap in hand, asking for help."

"I did no such thing." He rose from the chair.

"You did. You need me to solve this case for you."

He glowered at me. "I don't need anything from you, Watson! Just tell me what you've got."

"Those are two entirely contradictory statements," I said, then rapped my knuckles on the desk. "And my advice for you is to give Mr. Sinclair more attention."

"Who is this Sinclair guy you keep talking about?" Brown asked, lifting his nose.

"That's for you to find out," I said, rising from my desk. I stuck my phone in the pocket of my shorts, then walked to the door and held it for him. "Have a good evening, Brown. Good luck."

"I don't like your tone," he said, as he swept past me.

"Remind me who asked," I called after him. He slammed the door on his way out.

Aggy guffawed and followed me into the empty reception area. "He's awful. I'm sorry, Christie."

"He gave me exactly what I needed."

Twenty-One

The following morning...

I SPENT AS MANY DAYS IN THE OFFICE AS POSSIBLE —it helped me feel in control even when I wasn't—and sunny Friday mornings were no exception. I had arranged to meet up with Aggy at the local bakery to start our day. She loved soaking up the ambience, given her plans to own a bakery one day, but when I arrived at Dolores' Bakery, she wasn't waiting in line.

Thoughts of the case consumed me while I waited for her to show up.

Investigator Brown had suggested that Simone had an

alibi for the night of the murder, but he hadn't given me details about what that alibi could be.

If Simone wasn't the killer, my two other suspects had to come into sharper focus. Noel, who had hated his sister and denied any relationship with her, and Gordon, who had been her therapist and had closed off his file with her.

Could that have been by design? A plan to make it seem like he had referred her to another therapist, when he had wanted to kill her? But what was the motive and where was his sudden connection to Mona coming from?

I shuffled through the bakery, until I reached the front of the line.

The hustle and bustle of people chattering in the line or the bakery itself, the hiss of the coffee machine, brought me back to the present with an unpleasant bump.

Aggy hadn't shown up.

"What can I get for you?" the barista asked, with an air of having to repeat herself.

I blinked. Where the heck was Agatha?

"Sorry," I said. "Nothing at the moment." And then I dipped out of the line and exited the bakery, whipping my phone out as I went.

I called Aggy's number. The phone went to voicemail immediately. It was off.

"Agatha," I said. "Where are you? Call me as soon as you get this." My pulse raced. *No way. No way.*

If the Somerville Spiders had decided to strike...

But I'd made contingencies for this, purposefully. I'd installed a parent's tracking app on her phone that worked off GPS. I strode through town, heading back toward the office building, barely hearing the greetings from townsfolk as I went.

Agatha's last tracked location had been recorded this morning at 06:30 a.m. in front of a building on Fifth Street. Mona Jonah's Gossip Shoppe.

Anger flushed my face with heat.

I sprinted down the sidewalk, pocketing my phone as I ran toward the building. If Mona had done something to her, I'd make her rue the day she'd glanced in Agatha's direction. *Why would Mona do anything to her? It's not her style.*

I pushed past people on the sidewalk, heedless of their cries, and burst into the gossip store. Gossip Circle members milled around in their ridiculous pink jackets, chatting and sipping coffee. There were a few regular townsfolk at the tables, reading Mona's gossip pamphlets. Aggy wasn't here.

A Gossip Circle member spotted me and came over, flicking her curls. "Excuse me," she said. "Can I, like, help you?" Her tone dripped with disdain. "Because this is a paid establishment. If you'd like a cup of coffee or a copy of the gossip column, then—"

I grabbed her by the front of her jacket and drew her toward me, ignoring her cry and the gasps from the other Gossip Circle members.

"Where is she?" I ground it out through my teeth.

The girl's bright green eyes flicked off to the left, where the office door was shut.

I let her go and strode toward it.

"You can't go in there!" she shouted. "You—"

I burst into the office, fully expecting Agatha to be inside. My anger fading into shock and then... *Gross.*

Mona and Gordon Sinclair were wrapped in a loving embrace, his hands splayed across the back of her Gossip Circle jacket and her sunglasses skew atop her head.

"Where is she?" I asked.

The pair sprang apart. Gordon had lipstick smeared across his lips, and Mona went red as a cranberry.

"What are you doing here?" Mona asked, gathering her coat and rearranging the auburn locks that circled her face. "How dare you burst in and—"

"Where's Agatha?" I asked.

"Agatha?" Gordon gave Mona a quizzical look.

She flicked her crimson nails at him, dismissively. "You must have lost what's left of your mind, Watson." Embarrassment fading, Mona was coming back to herself. "Why would I know where your wretched cousin—"

I took a step toward her, and both Mona and Gordon backed up at the look on my face. "Don't you say a darn thing about her," I said. "Where is she? I know she was here."

"She might have been hanging around this morning," Mona said. "But I haven't seen her since then. She left."

I searched her face for any hint of a lie and found none. I walked out of the office.

"Watson!" Mona yelled. "Watson, what's wrong with you? You can't go around bursting into people's offices and—"

I exited the building and strode up and down the street, checking alleyways and storefronts, stopping at the wedding planner's boutique, in case she'd gone in there. Bertrand smiled and waved at me from inside, and I gestured to the door.

"Good morning, Miss Watson," he said. "Did you have a question about the wedding?"

"Have you seen my cousin, Agatha Dupin, this morning?"

"No," he said. "She's the redhead who wears those fabulous hats, yes?"

I nodded.

"I haven't seen her. Do you need me to—?"

I waved him off with my thanks then started back up

the street. Where had Agatha gone? Or worse, who had taken her? Next on my list of places to check was the Burger Bar, but I wasn't sure that made sense—why would Agatha have turned off her phone to go for lunch or breakfast? She wouldn't have.

What if the Spiders snatched her?

Where was Special Agent Roberts? Why had she darn well disappeared when I needed her the most?

I entered the Burger Bar and found it empty—it had just opened. Grizzy smiled at me from behind the counter, giving me a wave. Her face fell. "What's wrong?"

"Agatha's missing," I said. "I can't find her. I need to call the cops."

Grizzy's hand flew to her mouth. "Oh, Christie, I'm sorry. You don't think...?"

"That's exactly what I think. I don't know what the alternative could be," I said. "You haven't seen her this morning, have you?"

"Only briefly. I saw her walk by on her phone, heading in the direction of Fifth Street."

Which checked out, since that was her last location. I didn't want to call Hardwick and get him involved, but without Roberts around, I didn't see that I had a choice. Every moment counted in finding a missing person. I'd have to tell Hardwick that Aggy was missing, but not the details about the Spiders, in case he was a plant himself. I couldn't trust anyone except those I cared about.

Grizzy circled the counter and came over. "Don't worry, Chris. We'll find her."

I burst into tears, and my best friend drew me into a hug.

Twenty-Two

Later that afternoon...

MY TEARS HAD DRIED LONG AGO, REPLACED BY frustration. I'd touched base with Missi and Vee, who were on the hunt for Agatha themselves, spreading news through Sleepy Creek that she hadn't been seen since the morning.

Hardwick had been unhelpful. He'd refused to report her as a missing person until twenty-four hours had passed, and he didn't understand my urgency, nor could I explain it to him.

I'd spent the day walking through the streets of Sleepy

Creek, searching for Agatha, until, eventually, I'd returned to the office to take a short rest.

She had to be alive. I wouldn't allow any alternative.

I stared at my phone, willing it to ring.

A text blipped through on the screen, and my heart flipped. Aggy's name popped up, along with a message.

> I'm fine.

My eyes widened.

I tried to call her. The phone rang two times before Aggy hung up on me.

> Seriously, Christie, I'm fine. I have to do things that you don't have to worry about.

> What does that mean?

> It's a secret.

> Send me a picture so that I know you're okay.

A moment later, an image of my cousin popped through on my phone. She gave me a thumbs up, looking stern, and wearing her favorite Stetson, which obscured the background of the image, unhelpfully.

I'm switching my phone off again. I'll be back soon. Stop looking for me! It's important.

Aggy. This is ridiculous. You know how dangerous this is given the Spiders.

But my message went undelivered. Darn her and her crazy schemes. I made several calls in rapid succession, to Liam, Grizzy, and then to the twins to let them know the updates.

Afterward, I opened my kid tracking app and found her location.

She was on the outskirts of town.

At King Motors.

What on earth was my cousin up to? Trying to track down the killer by herself? I wouldn't put it past her, both because I was stressed and because she was always determined to prove herself. She wanted her inheritance badly.

But I wasn't going to let her do anything stupid and put herself in danger on my watch. I jumped out of my seat and headed out of the door.

ఌ

KING'S MOTORS WAS CLOSING WHEN I ARRIVED, and my cousin was nowhere to be seen. Agatha had either moved on because she'd realized that I would track her down, or she was hiding close by. I scanned the parking lot from my Corvette, watching as the salesmen closed up shop for the day.

The guy who'd been interested in Agatha drove off in a Honda, his cheesy smile missing, replaced by bouts of continuous yawning.

Noel King stayed behind the longest, talking on the phone and repeatedly checking the time on his flashy watch.

Where are you, Aggy?

The light had faded to gray, but it was as hot as it had been this afternoon, even with my car window rolled down to let in the chirping of crickets and the dull hum of traffic as people headed home after a long day of work.

I kept my gaze on Noel.

After another half an hour of pacing, he exited the building and headed for a flashy black SUV. Noel drove off, and, on a whim, I started my Corvette and followed him.

Mr. King didn't head in the direction of his house on Downtown Street but headed into town instead. He drove past the Sleepy Creek park and took several back roads until he parked outside the Sleepy Creek High School.

I drove past him and parked around the corner, out of sight.

What was Mr. King up to? Why hadn't he gone home and why come to the high school of all places? The kids had their summer vacation at the moment, so it wasn't like he was picking up a son or daughter from school, and Mona's gossip rag had claimed he was an eligible bachelor.

By the time I rounded the corner, Noel was halfway to the school auditorium, carrying a violin case.

A violin case.

Did the instrument belong to Elodie? Was he trying to get rid of evidence?

I watched as Noel entered the side doors and they clapped closed behind him. I hurried up to the auditorium, peering through the windows.

Noel had taken a seat among several other adults, all of them holding violins. A woman stood near the front of the group, holding a violin of her own. She smiled at the group and brought them to order.

A violin class. He's taking night classes in violin.

On a Friday. At the school.

I checked the time, and my eyebrows crept upward. Depending on how long these violin classes were, and whether there'd been one on the night of the murder, this might provide Noel with an alibi.

But it was odd. He didn't strike me as the type of guy who played violin.

And he had despised his sister. This instrument was a connection to her. I backed into the darkness and leaned against the brick wall, warm from the summer's day, and settled in to wait. I wasn't going to find out any of these answers without talking to the man.

An hour later, the auditorium doors opened and the students emerged, chatting to each other. Noel was at the back of the group, and I separated from the shadows and tapped him on the shoulder.

"Mr. King," I said. "Can I have a minute of your time?"

He spun toward me, bringing up the violin case and holding it out to protect himself. His expression dropped into a scowl. "You again," he said. "What do you want?"

"The truth," I said. "You're hiding from yourself, from this town, and from what happened to your sister, Noel."

"I told you, I don't know—"

"Elodie was your sister. You don't have to lie about it. You don't even have to have liked her, but denying that she's related to you makes you look suspicious."

"I don't care what you think," he said. "Everyone in this town likes me."

"That can change," I said.

"Is that a threat?"

"No. Look, the detective who's in charge of investigating your sister's murder is a hack, and the private eye that's assisting him is unimaginably inept. You don't want them digging into your business and deciding you're their person of interest if you had nothing to do with this."

He stared at me, unspeaking, but his gaze softened.

"Why the violin?" I asked, hoping to establish rapport with him. "Because it's challenging?"

"Because my parents don't approve of it," Noel said. "Just like they didn't approve of Elodie or anything that wasn't according to the plan for our family." The words burst out of him, like a dam breaking after years of disrepair. "I've done everything they've ever wanted of me. Everything. I've played the part, made money for our family, but the pressure never ends. They want more. Always more. And this... this is my way of fighting back." He wriggled the case.

The teacher exited the auditorium, brushing gray curls behind her ear with a slender hand. "Do you need anything, Noel?" Her tone was pointed.

"I'm fine, Tisha, thank you."

She retreated, but not before she'd given me a purse-lipped onceover.

"I had to do what Elodie couldn't," Noel said. "I had to carry my parent's expectations, while she was free of them. And yes, that meant that she didn't get an inheritance, but she was free. For what it mattered, though she couldn't come to terms with it."

"You were here on the night she was murdered, weren't you?"

"Yeah." He swallowed. "She was—"

Sirens whooped in the street.

Twenty-Three

DETECTIVE HARDWICK MARCHED TOWARD NOEL King, his hand on his belt and an eyebrow raised. He'd parked his squad car outside the school property right behind Noel's SUV. Investigator Brown emerged from the squad and stood watching, his arms folded and an almost-comical smirk twisting his lips, visible thanks to the lights of the nearby lampposts.

"What's going on, Detective?" I asked.

Hardwick sneered at me. "I guess I should have expected to find you here, Watson."

"What is this?" Noel asked, glancing from me to Hardwick and back again. "Is this a set up?"

"Trust me, I had no idea that Hardwick would be here," I said. "If I'd known, I would have stayed in my office."

"I wish you had," Hardwick said, then turned to Noel. "Mr. Noel King, you're under arrest under suspicion of murdering Elodie King. I'm going to need you to turn around and put your hands on that wall." He gestured to the bricks beside the auditorium door.

"Are you crazy?" Noel asked.

"He has an alibi, Hardwick," I said. "He was here."

The detective ignored me and took a step forward. "Now, Mr. King, or I'll have to make you."

Noel glared at him, but turned around and faced the wall. Carefully, he placed his violin case on the floor beside him, and then he put his hands up.

"You've lost it," I said. "You've actually lost it."

"Get out of here, Watson, before I arrest you for interfering in my investigation."

This wasn't right. Either Hardwick knew something about Noel's alibi that I didn't or he had got it wrong. I had to talk to Arthur about this. I backed up, shaking my head, and bringing the keys to my Corvette out of my pocket, watching as Hardwick arrested an innocent man.

"I'll get you out," I called.

Mr. King might not be the nicest guy around, but he wasn't a murderer and he didn't deserve a life behind bars for a crime he hadn't committed. Nobody did.

I ARRIVED AT GRIZZY'S HOUSE AND FOUND MY friends seated around her kitchen table. Arthur wasn't home—I'd have bet he was at the station, given that they had a suspect in custody and would likely have to interrogate him.

Noel was smart and rich enough to get a lawyer that wasn't a public defender. He'd be fine without my help, but after the day I'd had, I needed a win.

"Anything else from Agatha?" Vee asked, as I took my place at the table.

"Not since that picture she sent me." And then I told them about the arrest and Brown's presence.

"You're sure it's not him?" Missi asked.

Grizzy stirred a sauce on the stove for tonight's dinner —chicken, gravy, and greens—tilting her head toward us as we talked.

"He has an alibi. And so does Simone, according to Investigator Brown, but how far can I trust him? It's either her or Gordon Sinclair."

"I heard a rumor," Grizzy said, tapping her wooden spoon on the side of the saucepan.

"Well?" Missi prompted. "Don't leave us waiting in baited breath, Griselda."

"Simone is hosting a memorial service for Elodie tomorrow," Grizzy said. "I heard about it from Hedy. She's been invited."

"Where is it?" I asked.

"At Simone's house," Grizzy said. "I can ask Hedy to text you the details, if you want?"

"Yeah, please. Thanks, Griz. You're the best."

She sighed and brushed her fingers off on her apron. "I honestly just want this to all be over. Arthur's been busy, and he comes home stressed every night, and he leaves early. Oliver's always asleep by the time he gets home, and it's frustrating having to do this on my own."

I pulled a face. "I'm sorry, Griz. I should help you more."

"I don't mean it like that," she said. "I'm annoyed at the situation. I sound like a spoiled housewife."

"That's not fair," Missi said. "You have a business of your own too. And a child. Arthur needs to pull his weight."

"Oh, he does," Grizzy said. "I'm sulking because I don't get to see him as much. But I love how protective you are of me."

Missi smiled at her, a sweet moment in the sour this weekend.

"I bet it's not easy working with Hardwick either," I muttered.

"That man's name is a curse word in this house," Grizzy said. "Arthur hates him, and I've never known Arthur to hate *anyone*." He was similar to Grizzy herself, kind and always wanting the best for the people around him.

"I don't blame him."

"What about your cousin?" Vee asked. "I'm concerned about her behavior."

"That makes two of us," I said, "but I can't do anything about it until she comes home. She knows the risks, and I've got the feeling that she's trying to cook up an answer to the same puzzle we're working on. She wants to prove herself and solve the case. And help. In her own way."

The conversation continued while Grizzy cooked dinner, and I sat back, mulling over the facts.

Aggy was missing. Special Agent Roberts was too. And now, Hardwick and Investigator Brown had made an arrest in the case that didn't make sense given what I'd discovered this evening.

Of course, Hardwick wouldn't want to hear it from me, but what if I told Arthur? Would that help?

I whipped out my phone.

> Arthur, sorry for bugging you while you're at work, but King has an alibi.

> You're kidding. When we interviewed him at the beginning of the week, he couldn't provide one other than to say he'd been at home sleeping.

Because he didn't want his parents to find out that he'd been playing the violin.

> He's got an alibi, Arthur. Push him for it. He was at the school auditorium on the night of the murder. Can you tell me anything about the case?

I'm sorry, but I can't do that.

> I understand.

I couldn't blame Arthur for denying my request. I didn't want him to wind up in trouble because of me, and it had been a desperate attempt to get a lead. I slipped my phone into my pocket and tried to enjoy the conversation with my friends, but how could I, given what I'd discovered?

"Anyone know anything about Sinclair?" I asked.

"He's a counselor with an attitude problem," Missi said. "Other than that, not really."

"He's dating Mona Jonah." It came out absently.

Missi did a spit take with her water, Vee recoiled, and Grizzy gasped.

"You're kidding me," Missi said. "You are kidding. He's at least ten years younger than her."

"That's ageist," Grizzy replied, hiding a smile.

"And ironic, given your obsession with Jarvis, sister," Vee added.

"Excuse me!" Missi grasped her chest. "I am not obsessed with anyone. I am a chaste, appropriate..."

The words trailed off, but the humor remained, and it uplifted my spirits. I needed all the goodness I could get. Tomorrow, I'd be crashing a memorial service.

Twenty-Four

AGGY HADN'T CONTACTED ME SINCE YESTERDAY, and her phone had remained shut off. My concern had grown significantly, but that picture she'd sent me had set me at ease. And I got the feeling that I'd run into her today.

She had a habit of showing up when I wanted her to stay out of my business, and today was a perfect opportunity for her to ruin my plans.

Simone's house, a shiplap double story with a mailbox bearing her last name, a picket fence, and a neatly kept lawn, had a line of Sleepy Creekers out front, wearing black. Looked like everyone in town had been invited, except for me.

Sleepy Creek was a close-knit community. Funerals,

memorials, and sometimes even birthdays were often considered town events rather than personal celebrations.

I parked the Corvette down the street, my curiosity growing.

Noel was off my list, which meant Simone had risen to the top.

She had been besties with Elodie, had recommended we go to the concert, and she'd dated Noel. She was intimately connected with the family. And Bertrand, our wedding planner, had dropped the news that she wasn't as close with Elodie as she'd claimed.

I took the steps two at a time and entered Simone's home. It was beautifully put together—polished tables, flower arrangements, and an open-plan downstairs where guests milled about, eating snacks and sharing memories about Elodie.

Though, how much they'd have to share was up for debate—she was new to town.

I searched the crowd of memorial-goers for Simone's familiar face, but she wasn't in the living room or kitchen.

A couple of people greeted me, and I nodded as I passed by.

She had to be upstairs.

I grabbed a glass of champagne and took the creaky, polished wooden stairs up to the second floor. Nobody stopped me. Why would they? I looked like I knew where I was going and what I was doing.

Upstairs was filled with the dull hum of chatter from the memorial service.

Voices drifted from a cracked doorway at the end of the hall.

"You can't be serious," Gordon said, in his nasal tones. "All of that, for nothing?"

I tiptoed toward the door, stopping a couple of feet away to listen in. I took my phone out of my purse and started recording, holding it at my side, innocuously.

"It's a mistake," Simone replied. "It's got to be, Gordy. Look, I'll call Mrs. King and ask her what's going on."

"Call her? That's a little obvious, don't you think?"

"What else can we do?" Simone's voice lifted. "Elodie would never have left me destitute. She loved me. I was her best friend."

"That's not the rumor that's floating around town," Gordon replied. "It's reached Mona's ears that you might have been on the outs with her. I'm telling you, if anyone finds out that things weren't peachy between the two of you—"

"Stop. Nobody's going to find out," Simone said. "And Mona's your problem, not mine. You keep your end of the deal, and we're good."

"What's the point if there's no pay-off at the end."

"Gordon, this isn't an issue. We got away with it. Noel's no longer a problem. We'll get our due, and then we can get back to our normal lives." Footsteps thumped across the flooring, and I backed up several steps then tossed the champagne onto my black blouse.

I grabbed the silk and held it out, grimacing and walking down the hall just as Gordon and Simone emerged from their clandestine meeting.

Simone stopped dead, eyes wide. "No guests upstairs!" she squeaked.

Gordon was pale.

"Sorry," I replied. "I couldn't find a bathroom. I'm such a klutz. I spilled champagne all over my blouse."

Simone stared at me, suspiciously. "You weren't invited."

"Huh?"

"You weren't invited to this party," Simone said.

"Memorial," Gordon corrected.

"Right, memorial. You weren't invited."

"It's Sleepy Creek," I replied. "Everyone's invited." I frowned. "Am I interrupting something? I—I just wanted to clean up." I tugged on my blouse, separating it further from my chest. It was drenched.

Gordon nudged Simone.

"Bathroom's right over there." Simone pointed to her left.

THE CHEESE BURGER MURDER

"Thanks. I'll be quick." I entered the bathroom and shut the door behind me, turning the key in the lock, and letting go of my blouse. I didn't care about the champagne mess. The two were conspirators.

The puzzle pieces fell into place.

Elodie had been killed for her potential inheritance. Simone had assumed that Elodie would leave her something in her will, and Gordon had thought that Elodie was wealthy due to their sessions. But Noel had told me the truth, Elodie couldn't come to terms with being estranged from her family.

It was horrible. Sad.

And the two vultures in the hallway had preyed upon a woman who needed help.

Gordon was broke. Simone was greedy, and poor Elodie had been an easy mark.

Gosh, it even made sense why Simone had dated Noel. Money. She'd wanted money.

I turned on the faucet in the bathroom and left it running while I sent Arthur the recording I'd taken.

> They killed her. What the heck was Simone's alibi? Brown told me she was accounted for.

> Mona, Gordon, and Simone were together on the night it happened.

> Mona lied. Mona lied about this because she's dating Gordon. Watch the recording, Arthur, and then get your butt over here!

A knock tapped at the door.

"Just a second," I said. "I don't have a shirt on." I splashed the water in the sink.

"Open the door, Miss Watson." Gordon rattled the handle.

"I told you," I snapped. "No shirt."

> I'm on my way over there. Keep them busy if you can, and then make yourself scarce, because Hardwick is furious.

> Furious that he's bad at his job?

> And at Mona.

> Something's got to give. Mona's got to be arrested for this.

But I had my doubts that it would happen. Hardwick was corrupt. We had to get rid of him, but that was a problem for another day.

"Open!" Gordon yelled.

I laughed under my breath and put my phone back in my purse. I removed my trusty pepper spray from it and readied my finger on the trigger. "I'll be out in a second," I said, and shut off the water.

Brace yourself.

I turned the key.

Gordon tried to enter the bathroom, his lips peeled back over his teeth. Simone was behind him.

I unleashed a stream of pepper spray into his face, and he screamed and doubled over, clawing at his eyes. Simone gasped and tried to make a run for it, but I sent a second stream in her direction, and she nearly fell over herself.

Man, I've got good aim. I hopped over Gordon, who was now in the fetal position in the bathroom entrance and grabbed hold of Simone.

She was standing, turning in circles, walking left and right like she didn't know what to do with herself, and if I didn't stop her, she'd fall down the stairs. While it was tempting to allow a murderer to meet an awful fate, Elodie deserved justice.

The commotion hadn't been noticed by the guests yet, but the screech of tires outside and the wail of sirens drew their attention.

Arthur and Hardwick had arrived. I sat Simone down then darted downstairs and into the crowd, hiding among them as the detectives strode through the entrance. I couldn't help smiling at the look on Hardwick's face. He would never live this down.

Twenty-Five

That night...

THE GROUP OF MY FAVORITE GIRLS, AND OLIVER, who was awake because he was teething, had gathered in Griselda's living room to celebrate. And to worry about Aggy, who hadn't turned up yet.

"That's that," Missi said, taking a bite of cheesecake. "This has to be the end of Mona Jonah. She's going to be arrested."

Vee pursed her lips. "Don't know about that. Detective Hardwick will find a way to let her off the hook."

"But how?" Grizzy asked, from where she sat on the living room floor, Oliver in her lap. My godson gnawed on a frozen banana, his little cheeks streaked with tears. "That's illegal."

"Arresting Noel without real evidence is illegal too," I muttered. "But he pulled that off. I don't know how he got a judge to grant him a warrant for that arrest without lying."

"Something has got to give." Missi was insistent. "We can't keep waiting for—"

The doorbell buzzed, and I got up. "That'll be Liam with the pizzas." I couldn't wait to see him. It felt like this week had been a blur of murder investigations, stress, and wedding planning.

I unlocked the door and lost my breath.

"Aggy!"

She stood on the front step, wet from head-to-toe for heaven alone knew what reason, her Stetson in hand, and a long-suffering expression on her face. Her glasses kept sliding down her nose repeatedly.

I threw my arms around her and squelched her against my chest. "Are you good?"

"Yeah," she squeaked. "I'm sorry, Christie. I wanted to solve the case and stop Brown from being so mean to you. That's all."

A figure stepped out of the darkness at the base of the porch stairs. Special Agent Roberts, wearing her busker get up, complete with a spangly shawl, smiled up at me. "I found her in the high school pool."

"Do I want to know why?" I asked.

"Because I called her name, she spooked, and then she climbed over the wall and fell into the water," Roberts said, and craned her neck for a glimpse of Grizzy's house. "You alone in there?"

"No." I fed Aggy into the house, and she was greeted by relieved shouts. Oliver started crying.

I shut the door and let them celebrate my hare-brained cousin's return.

"Where were you?" I asked, descending the steps to meet Special Agent Roberts.

"I was called away for an important meeting," she replied. "I had you being monitored the entire time."

I wasn't sure I believed her. "I told my friends."

Roberts released a breath. "I should have expected that," she said. "But that's fine. We'll do damage control where we can."

"And the Spiders?"

"I have my suspicions about a few new people in Sleepy Creek," she said. "But nothing you need to worry about yet. When you're in imminent danger, I'll let you know." And then Roberts turned to walk off.

"No."

"What?"

"No. You won't let me know. You'll keep me informed from now on," I said. "If you want my cooperation, give me something to cooperate with."

Roberts folded her arms. Her dangly earrings tinkled in the wind. "What do you mean?"

"I want contact with you. I want to know what's going on. I'm not going to live in darkness because you think it's what's best for me and my family."

"I know what's best—"

"You don't. You can't know, because you don't know us or this town. I was a detective, lady," I said. "I've worked in law enforcement. I understand protocol, and I understand when it's time to break protocol. Now is that time."

Roberts considered me for a moment, and then, finally, she nodded. "I'll pass it up the chain."

The gate clicked, and Liam came up the pathway, carrying an armful of pizza boxes. He greeted Roberts, and she gave him a tight smile before leaving without another word.

"What's that about?" Liam asked, giving me a kiss on the cheek. He smelled of the pizzeria and his leathery cologne—a smell I loved.

"The future," I said.

"I'm assuming that it's good news?" Liam asked.

I helped him bring the pizzas inside. "Sure," I replied.

"What else would it be?" Our friends greeted us and the pizzas with happy cheers.

❧

Hungry for more Sleepy Creek mysteries? Join Rosie's mailing list to find out when the next book releases, and you'll receive a free copy of two prequel books in the Burger Bar mystery series.

Head to www.rosiepointbooks.com to sign up.

Craving More Cozy Mystery?

If you had fun with Delta Mission, you'll, love getting to know Charlie Mission and her butt-kicking grandmother, Georgina. You can read the first chapter of Charlie's story, *The Case of the Waffling Warrants,* below!

"Come in, Big G, come in." I spoke under my breath so that the flesh-colored microphone seated against my throat picked up my voice. "What is your status?"

My grandmother, Georgina—pet name Gamma, code name Big G—was out on a special operation. Reconnaissance at the newest guesthouse in our town, Gossip. The reason? First, she was an ex-spy, as was I, and second, the woman who'd opened the guesthouse was her mortal enemy and in direct competition with my grandmother's establishment, the Gossip Inn.

Who was this enemy, this bringer of potential financial doom?

A middle-aged woman with a penchant for wearing pashminas and annoying anyone who looked her way.

Jessie Belle-Blue.

It was rumored that even thinking the woman's name summoned a murder of crows.

"I repeat, Big G, what is your status?"

"I'm en route to the nest," my grandmother replied in my earpiece.

I let out a relieved sigh and exited my bedroom, heading downstairs to help with the breakfast service.

In the nine months since I had retired as a spy, life in Gossip had been normal. In the Gossip sense of the term. I'd expected that my job as a server, maid, and assistant would bring the usual level of "cat herding" inherent when working at the inn. Whether that involved tracking down runaway cats, literally, or providing a guest with a moist towelette after a fainting spell—tempers ran high in Gossip.

What was the reason for the craziness? Shoot, it had to be something in the water.

I took the main stairs two at a time and found my friend, the inn's chef, paging through her recipe book in the lime green kitchen. Lauren Harris wore her red hair in a French braid today, apron stretched over her pregnant belly.

"Morning," I said, "how are you today?"

"Madder than a fat cat on a diet." She slapped her recipe book closed and turned to me.

Uh oh. Looks like it's time for more cat herding.

"What's wrong?"

"My supplier is out of flour and sugar. Can you believe that?" Lauren huffed, smoothing her hands over her belly while the clock on the wall ticked away. Breakfast was in two hours and Lauren loved baking cupcakes as part of the meal.

"Do you have enough supplies to make cupcakes for this morning?"

"Yes. But just for today," Lauren replied. "The guests are going to love my new waffle cupcakes, and they'll be sore they can't get anymore after this batch is done. Why, I should go down there and wring Billy's neck for doing this to me. He knows I take an order of sugar and flour every week, and I get it at just above cost too. What's Georgina going to say?"

"Don't stress, Lauren," I said. "We'll figure it out."

"Right." She brightened a little. "I nearly forgot you're the one who "fixes" things around here." Lauren winked at me.

She was the only person in the entire town who knew that my grandmother and I had once been spies for the NSIB—the National Security Investigative Bureau. But the news that I had helped solve several murders had spread through town, and now, anybody and everybody with a problem would call me up asking for help. A lot of them offered me money. And I was selective about who I chose to help.

"I'll check it out for you if you'd like," I said. "The flour issue."

"Nah, that's OK. I'm sure Billy will get more stock this week. I'll lean on him until he squeals."

"Sounds like you've been picking up tips from Georgina."

Lauren giggled then returned to her super-secret recipe book—no one but she was allowed to touch it.

"What's on the menu this morning?" I asked.

Lauren was the boss in the kitchen—she told me what to do, and I followed her instructions precisely. If I did anything else, like trying to read the recipe for instance, the food would end up burned, missing ingredients or worse.

The only place I wasn't a "fixer" was in the Gossip Inn's kitchen.

"Bacon and eggs over easy, biscuits and gravy, waffle cupcakes and... oh, I can't make fresh baked bread, can I?"

"Tell her I'll bring some back with me from the

bakery." Gamma's voice startled me. Goodness, I'd forgotten about the earpiece—she could hear everything happening in the kitchen.

"I'll text Georgina and ask her to bring bread from the bakery."

"You're a lifesaver, Charlotte."

We set to work on the breakfast—it was 7:00 a.m. and we needed everything done within two hours—and fell into our easy rhythm of baking and cooking.

My grandmother entered the kitchen at around 8:30 a.m., dressed in a neat silk blouse and a pair of slacks rather than the black outfit she'd left in for her spy mission. Tall, willowy, and with neatly styled gray hair, Gamma had always reminded me of Helen Mirren playing the Queen.

"Good morning, ladies," she said, in her prim, British accent. "I bring bread and tidings."

"What did you find out?" I asked.

"No evidence of the supposed ghost tours," Gamma said.

We'd started hosting ghost tours at the inn recently, so of course Jessie Belle-Blue wanted to do the same. She was all about under-cutting us, but, thankfully, the Gossip Inn had a legacy and over 1,000 positive reviews on Trip-Advisor.

Breakfast time arrived, and the guests filled the quaint dining area with its glossy tables, creaking wooden floors, and egg yolk yellow walls. Chatter and laughter leaked through the swinging kitchen doors with their porthole windows.

"That's my cue," I said, dusting off my apron, and heading out into the dining room.

I picked up a pot of coffee from the sideboard where we kept the drinks station and started my rounds.

Most of the guests had gathered around a center table in the dining room, and bursts of laughter came from the group, accompanied by the occasional shout.

I elbowed my way past a couple of guests—nobody could accuse me of having great people skills—apologizing along the way until I reached the table. The last time something like this had happened, a murder had followed shortly afterward.

Not this time. No way.

"—the last thing she'd ever hear!" The woman seated at the table, drawing the attention, was vaguely familiar. She wore her dark hair in luscious curls, and tossed it as she spoke, looking down her upturned nose at the people around the table.

"What happened then, Mandy?" Another woman asked, her hands clasped together in front of her stomach.

Mandy? Wait a second, isn't this Mandy Gilmore?

Gamma had mentioned her once before—Mandy was

a massive gossip in town. Why wasn't she staying at her house?

"What happened? Well, she ran off with her tail between her legs, of course. She'll soon learn not to cross me. Heaven knows, I always repay my debts."

"What, like a Lannister from *Game of Thrones*?" That had come from a taller woman with ginger curls.

"Shut up, Opal," Mandy replied. "You have no idea what we're talking about, and even if you did, you wouldn't have the intelligence to comprehend it."

The crowd let out various 'oofs' in response to that. The woman next to me clapped her hand over her mouth.

"You're all talk, Gilmore." Opal lifted a hand and yammered it at the other woman. "You act like you're a threat, but we know the truth around here."

"The truth?" Mandy leaned in, pressing her hands flat onto the tabletop, the crystal vase in the center rattling. "And what's that, Opal, darling? I'd love to hear it."

"That you're a failure. You sold your house, left Gossip with your head in the clouds, told everyone you were going to become a successful businesswoman, and now you're back. Back to scrape together the pieces of the life you have left."

"Witch!" Mandy scraped her chair back.

"All right, all right," I said, setting down the coffee pot

on the table. "That's enough, ladies. Everyone head back to their tables before things get out of hand."

Both Opal and Mandy stared daggers at me.

I flashed them both smiles. "We wouldn't want to ruin breakfast, would we? Lauren's prepared waffle cupcakes."

That distracted them. "Waffle cupcakes?" Opal's brow wrinkled. "How's that going to work?"

"Let's talk about it at your table." I grabbed my coffee pot and walked her away from Mandy. The crowd slowly dispersed, people muttering regret at having missed out on a show. The Gossip Inn was popular for its constant conflict.

If the rumors didn't start here then they weren't worth repeating. That was the mantra, anyway.

I seated Opal at her table, and she pursed her lips at me. "You shouldn't have interrupted. That woman needs a piece of my mind."

"We prefer peace of mind at the inn." I put up another of my best smiles.

Compared to what I'd been through in the past— hiding out from my rogue spy ex-husband and eventually helping put him behind bars when he found me—dealing with the guests was a cakewalk.

"What brings you to Gossip, Opal?" I asked.

"I live here," she replied, waspishly. "I'm staying here while they're fumigating my house. Roaches."

"Ah." I struggled not to grimace. Thankfully, my cell phone buzzed in the front pocket of my apron and distracted me. "Coffee?"

"I don't take caffeine." And she said it like I'd offered her an illegal substance too.

"Call me if you need anything." I hurried off before she could make good on that promise, bringing my phone out of my pocket.

I left the coffee pot on the sideboard, moving into the Gossip Inn's spacious foyer, the chandelier overhead off, but catching light in glimmers. The tables lining the hall were filled with trinkets from the days when the inn had been a museum—an eclectic collection of bits and bobs.

"This is Charlotte Smith," I answered the call—I would never get to use my true last name, Mission, again, but it was safer this way.

"Hello, Charlotte." A soft, rasping voice. "I've been trying to get through to you. I'm desperate."

"Who is this?"

"My name is Tina Rogers, and I need your help."

"My help."

"Yes," she said. "I understand that you have a certain set of skills. That you fix people's problems?"

"I do. But it depends on the problem and the price." I didn't have a set fee for helping people, but if it drew me away from the inn for long, I had to charge. I was technically a consultant now. Sort of like a P.I. without the fedora and coffee-stained shirt.

"My mother will handle your fee," Tina said. "I've asked her to text you about it, but I... I don't have long to talk. They're going to pull me off the phone soon."

"Who?"

"The police," she replied. "I'm calling you from the holding cell at the Gossip Police Station. I've been arrested on false charges, and I need you to help me prove my innocence."

"Miss Rogers, it's probably a better idea to invest in a lawyer." But I was tempted. It had been a long time since I'd felt useful.

"No! I'm not going to a lawyer. I'm going to make these idiots pay for ever having arrested me."

I took a breath. "OK. Before I accept your... case, I'll need to know what happened. You'll need to tell me everything." I glanced through the open doorway that led into the dining room. No one looked unhappy about the lack of service yet.

"I can't tell you everything now. I don't have much time."

"So give me the *CliffsNotes*."

"I was arrested for breaking into and vandalizing Josie Carlson's bakery, The Little Cake Shop. Apparently, they found my glove there—it was specially embroidered, you see—but it's not mine because—" The line went dead.

"Hello? Miss Rogers?" I pulled the cellphone away from my ear and frowned at the screen. "Darn."

My interest was piqued. A mystery case about a break-in that involved the local bakery? Which just so happened to be run by one of my least favorite people in Gossip?

And when I'd just started getting bored with the push and pull of everyday life at the inn?

Count me in.

Want to read more? You can grab **the first book** in *the Gossip Cozy Mystery series* on all major retailers.

Happy reading, friend!

More for you...

Sign up to my mailing list and receive updates on future releases, as well as **FREE** copies of *The Hawaiian Burger Murder* and *The Fully Loaded Burger Murder*.

They are short cozy mystery featuring characters from *the Burger Bar Mystery series.*

Head to my website to sign up:
www.rosiepointbooks.com

Or follow me on BookBub to find out when I release new books!

.

Printed in Great Britain
by Amazon